'You missed a bit.' Freya pulled off her mitten and brushed the corner of his mouth with the pad of her thumb.

It was an innocent gesture, but the moment she touched Lucas his whole body sparked to life, every nerve-ending tingling with awareness. As though he'd been dormant for too long, waiting for her to initiate that contact, that bolt of electricity, to awaken him from his slumber.

'Thanks.' He locked his eyes on hers and he saw the brief flare of desire before she blinked it away. They might only have been married a short while, but he knew his wife well enough to recognise that look. It was the same flicker of interest he'd found so hard to resist when they'd first started working together and he still didn't want to. He could see that same internal fight against it in her eyes too, and hope flared in his chest along with desire.

The most he'd thought he could ask from her was forgiveness, so he could start his new life. He had never imagined that the one good thing about his past might still be available to him. If he'd known there'd be the slightest possibility he could have his wife back in his life he would've done everything to make it happen once he was strong enough to fight for her again. He'd simply accepted that he'd hurt her too much ever to go back. Now he wondered if she might still harbour feelings for him somewhere beyond that tough shell she'd cocooned herself in.

Dear Reader,

Writing a Christmas book has been a dream come true for me. I am one of those people, like Freya, who still wants to believe in the magic of the festive season. My mum made it such a special time of the year that I never did want to grow up. Even when I'd left home and had children of my own she still managed to wrap up a slice of that nostalgia in a parcel of sweets, books and pyjamas for me to open on Christmas morning.

For us, the day was always about family. Even though she and my gran are gone now, the rest of us still get together for the traditional board games and obligatory game of bingo after we've stuffed ourselves with turkey sandwiches and chocolate.

Lucas is my Grinch, who doesn't understand the warm, fuzzy feeling of having family around at Christmas because he's never experienced it. Of course Freya and I have worked extra hard to show him how special it can be. And what better place is there to start than on a trip to see Santa Claus in Lapland?

Let's just hope it turns out better than *our* family visit there, with a toddler who hated the cold and has no memory of the trip at all…

Merry Christmas!

Karin xx

THEIR MISTLETOE BABY

BY
KARIN BAINE

Published in Great Britain 2017
By Mills & Boon, an imprint of HarperCollins*Publishers*
1 London Bridge Street, London, SE1 9GF

© 2017 Karin Baine

ISBN: 978-0-263-07020-0

MIX
Paper from
responsible sources
FSC™ C007454

This book is produced from independently certified FSC paper to ensure responsible forest management. For more information visit www.harpercollins.co.uk/green.

Printed and bound in Great Britain
by CPI Group (UK) Ltd, Croydon, CR0 4YY

Karin Baine lives in Northern Ireland with her husband, two sons, and her out-of-control notebook collection. Her mother and her grandmother's vast collection of books inspired her love of reading and her dream of becoming a Mills & Boon author. Now she can tell people she has a *proper* job! You can follow Karin on Twitter, @karinbaine1, or visit her website for the latest news—karinbaine.com.

Books by Karin Baine

Mills & Boon Medical Romance

Paddington Children's Hospital

Falling for the Foster Mum

French Fling to Forever
A Kiss to Change Her Life
The Doctor's Forbidden Fling
The Courage to Love Her Army Doc
Reforming the Playboy

Visit the Author Profile page at millsandboon.co.uk.

For my wonderful mum, who created the magic,
and my boys William and Alexander,
who still let me pretend it exists.

Thanks to Laura, Julia and Chellie for helping me
write the best Christmas story I could.

Praise for
Karin Baine

'The moment I picked up Karin Baine's debut medical
romance I knew I would not be disappointed with her
work. Poetic and descriptive writing, engaging dialogue,
thoroughly created characters and a tightly woven plot
propels *French Fling to Forever* into the must-read,
highly recommended level.'
—*Contemporary Romance Reviews*

PROLOGUE

THIS WAS GOING to be the best Christmas ever. Freya was going to make sure of it. She heard Lucas turning his key in the front door and hoped the smell of her home cooking would put a smile back on his face.

'I'm in the kitchen,' she called, thankful she'd had the day off to make up for their earlier tiff.

Lucas hadn't been in the best of moods lately, which surely hadn't been helped by having to work Christmas Eve or her mistake of bringing up obviously delicate subjects when he was overworked and overtired. Not that she'd expected the idea of having a baby to be so controversial for a doctor who'd chosen to specialise in paediatric care and was so great with his young patients.

They'd never discussed starting a family. Freya had simply assumed Lucas would be as keen as she was, but his negative reaction to the idea this morning had told a different story. He'd surprised her by storming off to the hospital, slamming the door behind him when she'd mentioned feeling broody recently. In hindsight, she had put him on the spot by asking when they could start thinking about babies when he was obviously under a lot of pressure already and not in the right head space to become a father yet.

They could discuss it properly later so they were both clear on the long-term plans for this relationship.

As Lucas strode into the kitchen, still wearing the same scowl he'd had for days now, Freya conceded it probably wasn't good timing anyway when marriage already seemed far from the fairy tale she'd always imagined. Her spirits sank a little as that dream of having a family of her own seemed further away than ever. Lucas's recent mood swings were even making her slightly regret the pact she'd made with him that they would spend the holidays together, just the two of them. This would be her first year not sharing it with her tinsel-loving, Christmas-aholic parents, made more difficult by the fact her new husband didn't appear to share her enthusiasm for the season either.

The more Freya tried to make it special for them, the more detached Lucas seemed to become, but she was determined to make Christmas, and their marriage, a success. She'd lost too much already to let it all slip through her hands again.

'You've been busy.' Lucas leaned up against the refrigerator and gave the baked goods lining the kitchen counter a cursory glance before he continued scrolling through his phone.

If Freya was honest, it wasn't the amorous reunion she'd been hoping for where they would both admit they'd been in the wrong and engage in some wild kitchen make-up sex so they could move on and enjoy the rest of Christmas.

She'd heard passion sometimes went off the boil when you got married but she hadn't expected it after only a few months. They should still be in that can't-wait-to-rip-each-other's-clothes-off honeymoon stage, which was why she was worried she wasn't living up to his wifely expectations. Her mother had always seemed to juggle her nursing career and her home life perfectly and she couldn't help but wonder if this blip in their love life had somehow been down to her. After all, she didn't have a good record for keeping men interested. All she wanted to do was make this first Christmas together special for him.

'The turkey's almost done if you want some. I always love Christmas Eve at home, with the smell of the turkey cooking and getting to sample some before dinner on the big day. I've made my own stuffing too, just the way my mum always did. Maybe I'll get to pass on the family tradition someday too.' It slipped out before she realised and she tensed, waiting for another heated reminder she was alone in her enthusiasm for a large brood to fill her house at Christmas.

'I'm not really hungry. Maybe later.' Luckily, Lucas appeared oblivious to her slip of the tongue, his phone still monopolising his attention. Freya told herself such was the nature of being married to a paediatric consultant—he was always in demand—but there was a niggling doubt something else was behind his recent distraction. Especially when there'd been a few occasions he'd seemed to end calls abruptly when she'd walked into the room.

'I made gingerbread men too. You know Christmas isn't Christmas without creating a cloned army of little dudes capable of breaking your teeth on the one day of the year a dentist is impossible to get hold of. I thought you could help me decorate them later in time for Santa Claus stopping by.' The ironic nod to her childlike obsession with the season had been an attempt to make him laugh but Lucas simply rolled his eyes as though it was a chore she was forcing him to perform, the joke lost on him. Freya made the excuse to herself that he was probably exhausted after his shift because it was less painful than believing he'd tired of her already.

'Great. I…er…think I'll go take a shower first.' He walked out of the kitchen, batting away the paper garlands she'd hung from the ceiling with his free hand, as if they were nothing but a nuisance.

That was exactly how she didn't want him to see her—as if she was nothing more than a pretty decoration he could do without cluttering up his life—but even when he wasn't working he came to bed late and rose early, so they spent little time together as a couple these days. Married life was new to them both but she would do whatever it took to make this work. This was her chance to have the family she'd always wanted and she wasn't going to fail a second time.

Lucas closed his eyes and let the water wash his tears away where no one could see them. As a newlywed spending his first Christmas with his beautiful wife this should have been the happiest time of his life. Yet he couldn't seem to get excited about their future when his past had come back to haunt him so vividly.

He couldn't begin to think of starting a family now when he was still reeling from the news of his father's death. The impact of losing the only parent he'd known had been greater than he'd ever imagined but not because he was grieving the loss of the man who'd raised him. His sorrow was for the childhood he'd been denied and the one he'd suffered instead. The one he now couldn't escape in his head and that wouldn't let him enjoy married life in peace.

Everything he had worked so hard to achieve seemed like a lie now that he was forced to face who he really was behind the career and success he'd built for himself. It wouldn't be fair to bring a baby into existence when he was struggling to hold his own together. He could never hope to give a child a happy, secure home now when his world felt as though it was crashing down around him.

Lucas scrubbed away his self-pity and shut off the shower. None of this was fair on Freya. A normal husband would've told his wife his estranged father had finally succumbed to liver disease and had someone to endure the funeral with him. He would have given her the reason he was so against the idea of bringing a baby into the middle of his personal turmoil—he was afraid of becoming his father's son and ruining another childhood. Except his relationship with his father had been so toxic he hadn't wanted the ugliness of it to taint her. Freya was so idealistic about their marriage and how the next phase of their life together should play out he didn't want to destroy that rosy vision with the disturbing reality behind his.

He should've known it would take more than time and distance to truly escape the man's clutches.

When Lucas had received the call about his father's passing, he'd been forced to think about the man he'd been and had instantly been transported to a time he'd done his best to forget. Now, every time he closed his eyes he was overwhelmed by memories he'd tried to suppress, until even his waking moments were dominated by dark thoughts and a need to escape them.

Freya was the only one saving him from total despair but he was drowning in his own misery and now, more than ever, she was drifting just out of reach as she fussed around, trying to make his house the home he'd never had.

Her talk of babies and family was only natural when he'd never spoken out against it but these past days had reminded him it was an impossible ask. Whilst his mind raged with the fear and injustice of his youth, he could never be the husband, or potential father, Freya assumed she'd married.

By the time he'd changed and come back downstairs she was plating up an early Christmas dinner for him to sample, but as much as he wanted to play along with this game of make-believe, the level of effort she'd gone to to try to please him only served to remind him of everything he'd missed out on. He could no longer force himself to fit into this kind of cosy Christmas scene since his father had managed to crash in and destroy the illusion. It was too late for him to find any enjoyment in it now. At this moment he didn't think he'd find joy in anything ever again.

'I thought we could each open an early present from under the tree. We always used to have a Christmas Eve present at home. Usually pyjamas.' Freya sat down at the opposite end of the dinner table still bubbling with excitement as though she expected Father Christmas to drop down the chimney any second. He'd never had any such delusions as a child or a grown-up.

'Sounds good.' If he'd known that was a thing he would've done a little more retail preparation to make her happy but this was all new to him. He'd never given much thought to gift giving other than a token gesture but the pile of presents she'd assembled beneath the tree would rival any window display on Edinburgh's Royal Mile.

'I know we'd planned a quiet day, but I thought maybe, if it's okay with you, we could drive over to my mum and dad's after lunch tomorrow. We've hardly seen them since the wedding.'

'I thought we were supposed to be spending it on our own?' Lucas's knife and fork clattered to the floor along with his stomach, the last of his appetite quickly disappearing. The last thing he wanted to do was spend the day with her seemingly perfect family when he'd just buried the only sorry excuse for a parent he'd ever had.

'I know. I just thought it might be nice to see them and break up the day a little…'

In that second he could see the disappointment in

her big brown eyes that he wasn't enough to make her happy. Christmas was a symbol of everything that was important to her—family. The one thing he'd learned to live without but which was everything to her.

Freya loved being with her parents, couldn't wait to be one herself, and he didn't want to be that dark shadow hanging over either her life or their child's, at any time of the year. What if he turned out like his father, unable to show any emotion other than hate? He was already on that path, distancing himself from his wife's love in the present to focus on the bitterness of his past. She deserved better than a man who wasn't strong enough to separate himself from a frightened little boy intimidated by his father.

Lucas rose from the table with a quiet acceptance he was no longer the man she'd agreed to marry and spend the rest of her life with, even if she wouldn't admit it. Their love might be physically keeping them together but it would ultimately tear them apart inside, forcing this relationship to work when they both wanted, needed, such different things.

'I'm sorry, Freya. I can't do this any more.' The words were ripped from his aching heart, leaving a hole in his chest he knew would never heal.

He couldn't be responsible for anyone else's life when he wasn't sure he wanted his own any more. It was getting too damn difficult to imagine a time when he would no longer be in pain and he didn't want the same for Freya or the child she expected them to raise in this mess.

This was the only way to save them both, even

though it might seem like intolerable cruelty tonight. It was painful now but hopefully, with time, Freya would realise it was the right thing for him to do. She was young and idealistic, with the kind of open heart that would help her find love again, where his had been flawed from the start. He'd never been able to fully give himself to her or the relationship when he'd been holding back the truth about his parentage.

'Lucas? I'm sorry… We don't have to go if you don't want to… Lucas?'

He got as far as the door before he heard her quickening footsteps behind him in the hallway but he daren't look back. His knees were already weak, his chest so unbearably tight that he couldn't even trust himself to speak without collapsing to the floor.

Leaving was the best present he could think of to give her. She could still have all those things she wanted, just with someone else. He'd be a lost cause for ever when he was walking away from the best thing that would ever happen to him but he should never have expected to have everything he'd ever wanted.

His father had been right all along. He was a useless waste of space.

CHAPTER ONE

Ten months later

FREYA ADJUSTED THE jingle bells on her hat, straightened her elf ears and pulled up her stripy stockings. Christmas was supposed to be the most wonderful time of the year and she was determined to make sure of it for the kids of Princes Street Children's Hospital. It didn't matter a jot it was only October when they were on their way to Lapland to see the beloved man in the red suit. While she was there she'd make sure to remind him he owed her big style for last year.

'Feeling Christmassy yet?' Gillian, her nursing colleague from the emergency department and fellow elf for the weekend, came to join her at the front of the plane to welcome on board the excited children and volunteers along with the flight staff.

'I'm doing my best.' It was difficult to get into the spirit since everything she'd once loved about this time of year now reminded her of her husband walking out of their marriage and the worst period of her life. However, this wasn't about her, so she plastered on the jolliest smile she could muster and handed out candy canes with a 'Merry Christmas!' to the special group of sick children the hospital had chosen for the charity trip.

'Well, you certainly look the part.' Gillian gave a little wolf whistle that had Freya tugging on the furry white hem of her green velvet dress.

'I knew it was too short. That's what happens when you're forced to shop in the kids' department.' Everything in the costume store had swamped her petite frame but she guessed her height was the reason she'd been chosen to be one of Santa's helpers in the first place. Well, that and her extensive nursing experience, which made her a vital part of this group.

Without a very skilled medical team these poorly children would never get to leave Edinburgh. Such was the seriousness of some of their conditions there were a few of them who rarely left the hospital. That was why this trip was so magical, so important to the families and to her when she saw many of them time and time again in the emergency department. She would simply have to set aside her own heartache and loneliness around the season to make this memorable for everyone.

'You look gorgeous. With any luck you might even catch the eye of a reindeer herder over here and decide not to come back.'

Freya was forced to bite her lip until the young passengers were out of earshot. There was no room for disappointment or disillusionment on this trip and her love life definitely fell into those categories.

'Men are definitely off my wish list for the foresee-able future. I barely survived the last one. All I want for Christmas is to forget about Lucas Brodie and remind myself I'm Freya Darrow—the woman who is Christmas personified, not some sad and lonely divorcee who spent last year crying into her eggnog.' So they weren't officially divorced, but since she hadn't seen Lucas again from the moment he'd walked out on her, Freya had eventually had to accept the marriage was over. She'd reverted back to her maiden name when she'd decided to rid all traces of him from her life once and for all.

In those heady days of their intense romance, she supposed they'd never taken the time to find out about each other beyond who they'd become as a couple. So physically wrapped up in each other and the idea of being together to care about anything else, they'd left no space for her to confide in him about the loss she'd suffered as a teenager or for him to share his apparently opposing views on starting a family. During the early days of their marriage she'd been so happy she hadn't wanted to spoil anything by reopening the old wounds of her past, naively believing everything would simply fall into place.

Then, when Lucas's moods had become unpredictable, she'd been afraid to upset either of them any more by bringing up the issue, unaware that while she'd been making plans for a family he had already been plotting an escape route. He'd given up on them before even admitting there'd been a problem; without even trying to resolve whatever issue which had been so great he'd seen no other option rather than to leave. It made her doubt if the strength of her feelings for him and investment in their relationship had ever been reciprocated.

'I'm glad to see you back to your old self but, ah, there is something about Lucas I should probably tell you...'

'I don't want to know. I'm only thinking happy thoughts this weekend.' Freya refused to let further mention of him steal what little there was left of her enthusiasm for the season and shoved the end of a candy cane in her mouth for a peppermint sugar hit. The rumours Lucas was back, working in their sister hospital across the city, had reached her ears too but she didn't want to think about it. Not now when she was just starting to pull her own life back together.

It wasn't so long ago she'd spent Christmas making tearful phone calls around hospitals and friends, trying to find out if he was even still alive. There'd been several days of sheer panic and disbelief before she'd heard he'd gone on sick leave from work and didn't want to be contacted. Apparently that had included her. To this day she still didn't know if there'd been someone else, or if her talk of starting a family had made him have serious second thoughts about spending the rest of his life with her. He hadn't done her the courtesy of ever explaining himself. Not that it would change what had happened now when she was finally trying to move on.

There was no way she'd let memories of her absentee husband spoil things now after she'd spent the week overdosing on schmaltzy Christmas films and hot chocolate in an attempt to recapture her love of the season again. This trip to the Arctic Circle was just what she needed to restore her faith in human nature and awaken her inner child. Plus it was a bonus to embrace every tacky, glittery bauble associated with the spectacle Lucas had despised so much.

'Merry Christmas,' Freya repeated to every little soul as they were helped on board, ashamed she was even thinking about herself today. This was a break from reality for all of them. Even the parents and siblings left at home would enjoy some respite themselves this weekend with a getaway in the Scottish countryside funded by the charity. It made a change for everyone whose lives normally revolved around hospital appointments and stress.

'Is Santa here yet?' A particularly eager young man ran down the aisle in search of the man in red.

'I told you, Sam, we see Santa at the *end* of the trip. Try not to get yourself over-excited before we even leave Scotland.' The volunteer assigned to him followed down the aisle, clutching an asthma inhaler in her hand.

'Someone's keen.' Freya loved the enthusiasm, even though it was a tad premature. They had a whole itinerary to keep tiny spirits up until they reached Santa's grotto deep in the winter wonderland of the Finnish forests. The excitement was catching already and she couldn't help but hope for a little magic herself by the end of the weekend. A memory swipe of her ill-advised workplace romance and an embarrassingly short marriage should do it. Failing that, she was a sucker for cuddly toys.

'His mum said he's been looking forward to this for weeks.' Young Sam and his aide took their seats and Freya could almost feel the sense of relief as well as expectation from everyone. This was an escape into fantasy and a chance for them all simply to be children again.

'Oh, to be that young and carefree again,' Freya whispered after them, hankering for the life she'd had before a runaway husband had left her so jaded and cynical.

'I really think you should know...' Gillian tried again to force the shadow of Lucas over the proceedings and she was wondering if her friend was trying to tell her he'd been spotted with another woman. After such a lengthy separation it was really none of Freya's business who Lucas might have hooked up with in the interim, or who he might see in the future, but the pain was still too raw for her to find out for sure. It had made it impossible to go and confront him at work when she'd heard he was back. She couldn't face seeing him, knowing he was happier without her, when she'd been broken into a thousand pieces without him. His reluctance to come to her and explain his whereabouts for these past months said everything about his complete disregard for her feelings.

'I think that's everyone on board now. We should find our seats for take-off. Once we're safely up in the air and the captain gives us the go-ahead we can organise the in-flight entertainment.' With virtual fingers in her ears, she put her head down and took her seat near the front of the plane, which was thankfully on the opposite side from Gillian's. She didn't want to spend the next few hours listening to a running commentary on her ex's exploits since he'd returned from the wilderness. Left with no other choice, Gillian huffed out a breath and buckled herself in across the aisle.

The lovely smiley member of the cabin crew who'd helped them decorate the inside of the plane with tinsel patted Freya on the knee to get her attention. 'We're just waiting for one more to arrive. Then we'll close the doors and really get this party started.'

'Of course. We wouldn't be going very far without the doctor, would we?' She prayed there wasn't some sort of medical emergency holding up the very man who'd be coordinating the children's medical care. They'd already had one of the non-medical volunteers pull out, leaving them short-handed. As lead nurse she'd agreed to supervise two of the children herself but they really couldn't do without the doctor.

'They've just called from the departure gate to say he's on his way now.'

At least the delay meant she could take a breather for a little while before she had to face her next challenge. Take-off was the one part of the flight experience she never enjoyed. That moment when the plane left solid ground and the world grew ever smaller beneath her was always a nail-biter.

She settled back in her seat and attempted to relax. From the moment they were up in the air until the time they landed back in Scotland, there wouldn't be much time for her to rest.

'Ladies and gentlemen, we have our last passenger

on board, so we can close the cabin doors and prepare for take-off.' The announcement was made as a wind-swept figure dashed on board and received a round of applause and a chorus of cheers.

Not from Freya. She was dumbstruck. Too trauma-tised to even remember how to breathe.

Lucas.

Here.

Now.

Unless she was having some sort of sugar-induced hallucination, he'd just stepped onto the plane.

'Sorry I'm late. Car trouble.' The late arrival shook the rain from his thick blond hair. Freya blinked as the water droplets showered over her and she was forced to face the fact her ex-husband was *actually* here. Not only that, he had the nerve to smile and breathe as though he'd never crashed her whole world around her.

She turned, open-mouthed, towards Gillian, who simply shrugged and mumbled, 'I tried to tell you.'

'Not hard enough,' Freya hissed. This couldn't be happening. She had no desire to see him or talk to him, not since it had become apparent he'd abandoned her and their marital home, and now he was here, gate-crashing her weekend away? That was cruel even by his standards.

'The doctor who was supposed to be travelling with us took ill. I only found out myself this morning that Lucas had been drafted in to take his place.'

'That still gave you time to tell me.' Now the doors were locked, she was shut in this very small, very pub-lic space with him. It wasn't the ideal place to face him for the first time in nearly a year when her emotions were bubbling so close to the surface they could very well blow out the doors of this aircraft. She was already hyperventilating; each gasping, shallow breath making it a possibility she might just pass out. That really would be the sour cherry on top of this mess.

'I didn't want to upset you or force you to back out. I'm sorry you've been put in this position. I know it's not fair on you, but we need you here.' Gillian wasn't the kind to employ emotional blackmail to get what she wanted and Freya knew she'd only done what she thought was best in the circumstances. If she had been aware Lucas was going to be part of this, she might never have made it on board the plane herself and that would have put the entire trip in jeopardy. It didn't make the prospect of spending enforced time with him any more palatable, though.

'It should've been my decision to make,' she grumbled, letting Gillian off the hook and directing her annoyance at the person who deserved it most. Lucas.

This volcano of bubbling emotion inside her was exactly the reason she hadn't wanted any contact with him. It was difficult to restrain herself from getting up and punching him in the face for running out on her the way he had or squaring up to him and demanding answers she probably wasn't ready to hear. Neither option would settle her again now when the mere sight of him was still enough to make her heart beat a little faster. Memories, good and bad, flooded back so quickly, so intensely she had to forgo her candy cane to reach for the little paper bag in the seat pocket to breathe into.

In.

Their first kiss on a night out with colleagues after weeks of working side by side when he'd been called in for cover in Princes Street and she'd been trying to ignore the growing attraction.

She'd never anticipated any sort of workplace romance, especially when he'd only been at the hospital on a temporary contract. That hadn't seemed the ideal basis for any long-term relationship, and she wasn't the type of woman who would ever find satisfaction in a fling, but he'd been so kind and attentive, to her and his patients, he'd eventually become the exception to her rule. Her gamble in letting her heart rule her head again seemed to have paid off since they'd kept dating long after his posting had finished, but she was still paying the price for her mistake now.

Out.

Lucas on one knee, promising he'd love her for ever and making her believe this time an engagement would mean marriage and a family and everything that had been taken from her in the past.

She'd made no secret of the fact she wanted the same kind of special relationship her parents had one day and had thought he'd understood how sacred marriage was to her, not something to ever be taken lightly. The proposal, over a candlelit dinner at his place, had been perfect because it had been a private moment between the two of them, somewhere she hadn't felt under pressure. The homely, romantic gesture had held more meaning to her than a scripted display of bravado in front of a crowd, and he'd made her believe he held the same values. Only to toss her aside when he'd grown tired of married life all too soon.

In.

Their wedding day, when she'd been on top of the world and had truly believed they'd be together for ever.

It had been a small church wedding since Lucas had had no family he'd wished to invite to the service. He'd looked so handsome, and had seemed so utterly devoted to her during their vows to one another, he would've rivalled any fairy-tale prince. During their first dance as husband and wife at the reception she would've even sworn he'd had tears in his eyes, but the adoration hadn't lasted.

Out.

The last image she had of him, walking out the front door only months later and breaking her heart in two.

That dream of her picture-perfect family had vanished along with him that day. He hadn't loved her enough to even work at their marriage, never mind raise babies with her. She guessed he'd decided somewhere along the way he hadn't wanted to follow that traditional love, marriage, kids route after all.

There'd been several self-centred men in her life since her first teenage infatuation, who'd run out on her when faced with the ultimate responsibility, but none of them had hurt her as much as Lucas because he was the one she'd never stopped loving.

The bag inflated and deflated in time with her shallow breaths.

'If you'll just take your seat, Doctor, we'll be on our way.'

Freya could hear the admiration in the young attendant's voice and an eerie sense of calm descended upon her. She'd been that naive girl once, dazzled by the handsome consultant with the pale blue eyes and the great smile. It had taken a lot longer for her to trust him with her heart. She'd mistakenly believed such a strong, reliable force in the workplace would make him the man who would be there for her when she needed him the most in her personal life too. The kind of man who wanted to settle down and would find contentment with a wife and a couple of kids. How wrong she'd been.

This past year had toughened her up and hopefully made her immune to those superficial charms now she knew he wasn't the man she'd thought he was behind the handsome facade. Lucas was no better than the first man who'd betrayed her trust. Perhaps even worse because he'd broken his vows as well as her heart.

She crumpled up the paper bag with much more force than was probably necessary and shoved it back in the pocket until she could dispose of it properly.

The one consolation she had in watching another woman fawn over him was seeing the smile fall from his lips as he made his way down the plane and spotted her sitting in the aisle seat.

'Freya?' He swallowed hard and Freya found some satisfaction that he didn't appear any more comfortable than she was with the situation. Even if this had been some sort of set-up to force her to talk to him, the reality might've actually made him face up to his actions. Nothing Lucas could say now would change what he'd done but dealing with the consequences might make him think twice about treating someone else with such scant consideration.

It didn't make the idea of spending the weekend in his company any more palatable.

'Lucas. You were the last person I expected to see,' she said through gritted teeth, hoping the disapproval was radiating off her. He was completely out of order, ambushing her like this, but it wasn't the time or place for a screaming showdown. No matter how tightly her fists were clenched or how raw her throat was with the effort of holding back tears and the urge to ask, *'Why?'* He didn't get to ruin any more of her life.

'I was asked to cover at the last minute…and I thought…' He was standing in the middle of the aisle, creating a bit of a spectacle as he blustered around her, attempting to squeeze his carry-on luggage in the overhead locker as the cabin crew tried to chivvy him to his seat.

'What? That this would make a good surprise?' If he was any good at reading body language, her folded arms and scowl should have told him otherwise. The fact that he'd chosen to play out this painful reunion in front of passengers and colleagues made matters worse. The one saving grace was that everyone else was so caught up in their own excitement the general ruckus on the plane should be drowning out this awkward conversation.

He ought to be on his knees again, begging her for forgiveness this time.

'Doctor, I really need you to take your seat as quickly as possible so we don't miss our flight slot.' The flight attendant flashed a warning through her too-bright, teeth-baring smile as she slammed the locker shut and ushered him to the seat in front of Freya's.

She gulped in a deep breath as he turned away from her and released her from the hypnotic trance of those too-easy-to-get-lost-in blue eyes. These months of tears and heartbreak hadn't managed to eradicate the strongest of all the emotions she felt for Lucas—love—and she hated herself for it as much as she wanted to hate him. She'd never asked for their relationship to end and it seemed her feelings hadn't diminished any over time. If she'd stopped loving him at any point during their separation it wouldn't hurt so much to see him again and be reminded of everything she'd lost.

This weekend was going to test her personally as well as professionally and turn her into a prisoner of her own emotions because absolutely nothing was going to spoil the magic for these children. Not even the unresolved issues of her marriage breakdown.

Lucas collapsed into his seat, the sight of Freya after all this time hitting him with the unexpected force of a runaway sleigh, even though he'd known she'd be here.

'Your seat belt, sir.' He was admonished by another member of the cabin crew as they completed

their safety checks and waited with increasing agita-
tion for him to buckle up.

'Sorry. So sorry.' He wanted to stamp the word in
bold black ink on his forehead so Freya could see it too
because he was seemingly incapable of vocalising his
regret for the way he'd left things between them now
they were face-to-face.

It had been nearly a year since they'd last seen each
other, yet her obvious pain, and his shameful guilt, felt
as fresh as if they'd only just broken up.

When he'd realised her name was on the staff list
he'd had second thoughts about volunteering for this
position, knowing a confrontation was inevitable. After
all, she'd loved him every bit as much as he'd loved her
before he'd abruptly ended their marriage. In the end,
he'd realised he had to man up and face her so they
could both have closure on that very difficult time in
their lives. It wasn't going to be easy to initiate a conversation about the possibility of divorce but a legal
end to their relationship was the next logical step if she
was ever going to be truly free of him and have the
fresh start she deserved. He'd intended to broach the
subject with her at some point on this trip when they
could talk more freely and once she'd got used to the
idea of seeing him again.

Except when he'd been planning his return to the
world, he hadn't filtered any residual emotions into
the equation.

The sight of her again had unexpectedly choked
him up, reminding him in that instant of everything
he'd lost to his illness. It was his friend Peter who'd

salvaged his career and liaised with the hospital during his sick leave but, ashamed of his weakness, he'd begged Peter not to reveal anything to Freya.

He'd had to jump through hoops with the hospital board to prove he'd recovered and get his job back, with numerous meetings and assessments with occupational health and the GMC before he'd been deemed fit enough to work. His colleagues and the senior consultants had supported his return, and now he was building up his hours at the hospital again, he'd managed to resurrect his career, but he'd known he'd never be able to win his wife back.

Seeing her again only increased that ache in his chest and suggested he wasn't ready to let her go just yet even when setting her free for good was the best thing he could do for her. So much time had passed he'd imagined they would both be glad to escape any ties to one another and he hadn't been prepared for the reaction of either of them upon seeing each other again.

His kind and gentle wife looked as though she wanted to physically hurt him. He'd always been able to read her because she never made any attempt to hide her feelings. Unlike him, who'd kept his secrets and emotions bottled up until he'd imploded from the stress of holding it all back and destroyed everything he'd ever loved.

Those almond-shaped eyes had flashed with wild fire when they'd lit upon him, full of anger and hurt. Arms folded as she'd confronted him, there'd been a hardness to her he'd never encountered before. Lucas wasn't naive or egotistical enough to have expected she'd welcome him with open arms but part of Freya's charm had always been her warm personality. It was a shock to the system to see her changed so much and it made him realise how much time had passed between them. It also made him question how much of that change was down to him.

In his mixed-up head he'd believed that by leaving her he was doing what was best, so he didn't drag her into that dark pit of despair with him. When his conscience did prick at the thought of her tear-stained face staring after him, he'd convinced himself she would've found someone else to replace him by now. That somehow leaving had been a selfless act on his part and she'd be cosied up with another man, planning the family she'd always wanted and he hadn't been convinced he could give her.

The reality was very different, of course, and made him see his actions through her eyes for the first time since he'd turned his back and left her to deal with the fallout alone. They'd been so in love but he'd shut her out to the point of ignoring her pain in favour of his own.

Even without her clipped tone and abrupt manner with him, Lucas could see the distress he'd caused in her defensive body language and it broke his heart. With the clarity of his recovery it was obvious now that walking away hadn't been the answer; he'd only caused them both further agony. At the time what had been left of his pride had decreed that he protect his new wife from the responsibility of knowing about his childhood and subsequent illness. It hadn't been her job to fix him. He'd had to fix himself. Now he was realising the extent of what that decision had cost him and Freya.

The plane rumbled down the runway and he instinctively reached back to give her hand a reassuring squeeze. He knew how much she hated this part of the flight.

'Are you okay?' He peered around the back of his seat to see her sitting bolt upright, her eyes wide with fear.

'I'm fine,' she snapped, and snatched away from his grip as though she'd been burned.

On their honeymoon she'd dug her nails so deeply into the armrest he'd thought she'd never let go as he'd tried to prise her off again, but she was letting him know now without doubt he'd given up that right to touch or comfort her any more. She was his wife in name only now and that was entirely his fault.

The tension in her body and her instant recoil was a stark contrast to the effect he used to have on her. That slightest touch brought back the torturous sights and sounds of their honeymoon and beyond, when she'd once melted beneath his touch. They'd been happy for a time, in love and in lust, and he wished it had never come to this when she'd rather suffer a panic attack alone than accept his help.

There was a long way to go to get her to hear him out and he had the distinct impression that if it wasn't for the people surrounding them she would tell him exactly what she thought of him without stopping for breath. There was a long list of his failings but he'd never been as aware of them as he was now when his sweet wife could barely control the rage she felt towards him. If he thought it would give either of them any satisfaction, or in any way make up for how he'd treated her, he'd offer himself up as a punch bag right now.

He mightn't have thought this through properly but he remained hopeful this weekend would provide an opportunity for him to explain himself and smooth the way for a talk about the next step. That was all he could ask and yet it was more than he probably deserved from her.

He listened to the *oohs* and *aahs* of the children as the plane soared upward and the city lights blazing through the dark morning gradually disappeared beneath the clouds. The minute they reached cruising height and the seat-belt light went out, the plane became a hive of activity again as people left their seats.

'So, ladies and gentlemen, boys and girls, who's looking forward to meeting Santa Claus?' The intercom crackled with the enthusiastic tone of a non-crew member and a quick glance confirmed it was the other elf he'd seen on board. Freya was on her feet too but she was handing out sheets of paper to the whooping passengers.

'We thought we'd get everybody warmed up with a few Christmas carols, so elf Freya is handing out some song sheets to everyone. If anyone wants to come up and sing a song or tell a joke while we wait, you're very welcome.'

Lucas managed to block out the tones of tuneless

childish warbling and recycled jokes because his attention was totally focused on Freya as she made her way through the cabin. That bright smile shone for everyone she spoke to and he held his breath, waiting for his turn; to feel her warmth upon him once again. Of course, it didn't happen. When she reached him the light dimmed in her eyes and the smile faltered.

'You're looking well, Freya.' It was the best he could come up with to fill the awkwardness of the moment but he meant every word of it. The passing of time hadn't diminished her beauty, or the effect it had on him. He still felt like the luckiest man in the world that she'd ever agreed to be his wife, and the stupidest for letting her go.

She turned to move on without saying a word but it had been so long since they'd been this close he couldn't help himself trying to prolong the moment.

'You've cut your hair.' The short, messy bob suited her fine features but he'd always loved her long chestnut-brown hair.

'I needed a change,' she said flatly, suggesting again there'd been more than physical alterations occurring in his absence.

His stomach rolled at the thought he'd been the cause of that sudden edginess to her when she'd always been such a bubbly, loving individual and his actions had hardened her heart the way his father's self-destructive behaviour had his. He knew what a long, painful process it was to get over that kind of damage and what it cost along the way. Not something he would ever have wished for Freya to go through, and exactly the reason he'd walked away in the first place.

'I am sorry. For everything.' Characteristically, he'd remained in denial until crisis point, when he'd been forced to witness the emotional effects of the damage he'd caused first-hand. While he had no desire to embarrass her in front of anyone here, it would be remiss of him not to acknowledge the wrong he'd done her, and if she chose not to speak to him after this flight at least he would know he'd made the apology and meant it.

'Perhaps you'd give us a song, Doctor? I'm sure the children would love it.' There was that smile again but there was no trace of friendliness in the way she'd bunched up the leftover song sheets in her fist. She was rejecting the apology as obviously as she could without drawing attention from the others because she would know taking part was the last thing he'd want to do.

Their marriage might've been short-lived but they'd been together long enough for Freya to know that this Christmas merriment was out of Lucas's comfort zone. Her enthusiasm for the season had been difficult to live with when he'd hated everything about it. The over-the-top glitter and expense was always a reminder of the childhood he'd been denied and the only reason he'd agreed to step in before he knew Freya was involved had been to ensure these kids had the happy memories he didn't.

'I…er…have a lot of paperwork to catch up on.' It wasn't a complete lie. As the emergency replacement for the usual medical coordinator, he'd been handed the itinerary at the last minute. Although he'd done his best to get acquainted with the case notes of the children who'd be under his care so there wasn't any room for error and he was fully prepared for any eventuality. Not that anything could've prepared him for this tense exchange but he deserved every bit of the hard time she was giving him.

'Well, don't let me take up any more of your time.' She made a move to leave but there was such resignation in her tone he didn't want her to think he'd ever dismissed her, or everything they'd ever had, as easily as it may have seemed.

He reached out to touch her arm but she flinched away from him again as though he'd given her an electric shock. A reminder of those early days when they'd been avoiding their growing attraction in the workplace, where every brush against each other had held so much meaning. The most obvious difference now was that she wasn't looking at him with undisguised desire, more like murderous intent.

'Don't be like this, Freya. I really am sorry...' If he'd been in her shoes he knew he'd probably never be able to forgive him either, but how could they ever resolve matters if she refused to be anywhere near him? Expecting a truce here was a big ask but eventually she might accept he was trying to make the best out of a bad situation. Perhaps a divorce would get that anger at him out of her system once and for all.

'If you'll excuse me, we have a very busy schedule ahead of us today and I wouldn't want to let people down.' Freya cut off his attempt to apologise again and put some distance between them, leaving the scent of cinnamon and peppermint lingering in her wake. She launched into the first rendition of an old Christmas classic, encouraging everyone else to join in and handing out percussion instruments to the youngest members of the party.

To everyone else sitting on this plane Freya was the life and soul of the party, bringing festive cheer to those who needed it most, but Lucas could see the brave face she was trying to put on. She refused to make eye contact with him again for the duration of the fun and games on board to pass the time for the children and he knew that determination not to let them down was because she'd been there. She'd been on the receiving end of bitter disappointment and broken dreams and it was all down to him.

His journey to recovery had come at Freya's expense and he couldn't fully move on from the past when it wasn't only his father who'd left a legacy of unhappiness behind. Unlike the man who'd made his life hell, he wouldn't be able to live with himself if he didn't try to fix things. Although he hadn't been able to provide Freya with the husband and family she needed or deserved, there was one thing he could give her that might go some way to making up for his behaviour. An explanation.

It wasn't going to be easy to open up about the demons that had driven him away or to get her to speak to him long enough to do so, but he owed it to her to try. Perhaps this visit to Father Christmas could give them both the gift they needed most—peace of mind.

CHAPTER TWO

'YOU LOOK LOVELY and cosy in there.' Freya was helping to dress the two little girls she'd been assigned for the duration of the trip in the ski gear and snow boots which had been waiting for the group at the other end of the flight.

It was daylight now and the quick peek they'd had from the plane at the snowy landscape had made them all keen to get out and explore but the subzero temperature meant they needed to be suitably dressed before they could venture outside. With the nature of the conditions a lot of the children were suffering it was doubly important they were all wrapped up against the elements.

Freya had changed out of her elf outfit and into her more suitable snowflake-adorned sweater and warm trousers before they'd left the airport. Even trussed up like the Abominable Snowman in this lurid pink ski suit she felt more comfortable; zipped in and covered up and hopefully protected from the penetrating stare of her ex-husband.

It had never entered her head that she would be

forced to face him on this trip but she'd been even more disturbed by the flutter of her pulse every time he looked at her. Something that had happened all too frequently during the flight for her comfort. She felt his eyes burning into the back of her head now, watching her with the intensity of a man who had something he needed to get off his chest. Whatever it was, she didn't want to hear it. Whether he wanted to salve his conscience and finally unload the reason behind his mysterious disappearance, or he was eventually attempting to claim back half of everything that was rightfully his, she wasn't going to do this in front of an audience.

Freya had been over every imaginable scenario in her head since he'd left her—from another woman to some sort of post-wedding jitters that had seen him running for the hills. In the end, it boiled down to the same thing—Lucas hadn't wanted to be with her any more and no amount of talking now could repair her shattered heart. Despite the thermal layers of clothes she couldn't help but shiver every time she thought of him reaching out to take her hand on take-off. The part of her that, apparently, hadn't endured enough humiliation wanted to believe it was more than some residual body memory making him reach out to reassure her. That, irrespective of everything, he still cared about her the way she obviously still cared for him. The wounded Freya, still recovering from her injuries, reminded her it wasn't possible given the way they'd parted and it wasn't healthy to hold out any hope otherwise. Such a weakness in her armour left her vulnerable to another attack on her heart.

'Where did my fingers go?' Five-year-old Hope waved her hand at Freya and pulled her back into the present fantasyland. She was one of several here with type one diabetes, which meant constant monitoring of her blood-sugar levels, to avoid highs and lows, and her activity levels. It left no room for daydreaming paediatric nurses.

'They're in there all snuggled together keeping warm. These are called mittens and all of Santa's visitors have to wear them so Jack Frost doesn't nip those little fingers.' She adjusted the mittens so Hope's thumbs made it into their own holes and gave her a bit more freedom of movement.

'Scarlett too?' She grabbed hold of Freya's other charge for the weekend, the look of concern for her friend's naked fingers clearly etched on her cherubic face.

At least it would make her job easier over the weekend if the two little girls were bonding and not pining for any siblings at home.

'Yes, Scarlett too.' Freya tugged another pair of mittens on, and with their matching cerise ski suits and woolly hats, they could've passed for sisters, twins even.

Her heart lurched at the sight of the two precious bundles whose lives had been entrusted to her for the duration of the trip by their parents. It was a great responsibility but also a huge privilege to be able to give them a taste of a normal childhood. She'd look after them as if they were her own. If things had worked out differently, the way she'd planned her life with Lucas, they could've been making this trip to see Santa with their own little ones.

That space in her heart echoed with sorrow as that image of her, Lucas and the babies she'd imagined they would have flashed into her head. She'd had so much love to give, ready to start their very own family, and he'd ripped it all away from her, leaving her with nothing. Looking after other people's precious babes was as close as she'd ever get to that mothering side again because she knew she'd never trust another man enough to ever start her own family now.

'So, this is Hope and Scarlett? Hi, girls. My name is Lucas and I'm going to be helping Freya look after you. If there's anything you need you just come to one of us, okay?' Lucas had managed to appear beside her without tripping her inner alarm warning and she bristled at having him so close, intruding on the moment. It didn't help when he was wearing a black beanie hat and electric-blue ski suit and looking like someone ready to have fun instead of a professional heartbreaker.

'Okay,' the girls chorused, nodding their heads, no doubt charmed already by the handsome doctor. He had that effect on people.

'It's time to get on the bus.' She ushered the girls out towards the waiting transportation that was going to take them on the first leg of their journey with more urgency now that he'd arrived on the scene.

That first blast of cold air was a shock to the system and she shooed the little ones up the bus steps so they didn't hang about outside any longer than was necessary.

'I only wanted to make sure you had Scarlett's anti-epilepsy drugs and Hope's insulin at hand. I'm checking off everyone's medication before we head out.' Lucas flipped through the paperwork he'd been studying on the flight as he'd avoided all the on-board activities, and unexpected heat burned Freya's cheeks at the mistaken belief his attention had been solely for her. Of course he'd be preoccupied with the treatment all of these children needed while they were here. It was his job to coordinate everything so they could travel safely. She would never question his professionalism. It was his cavalier attitude to his marital status she had an issue with.

'Yes, I have the AEDs, insulin and the times they've to be administered.' When it came to the care of her patients she took her job equally as seriously. She'd checked and double-checked everything these girls needed for the duration of this trip and wasn't leaving anything to chance. Although neither epilepsy nor diabetes were the sort of conditions that necessarily ran to a schedule.

'Good.' He gave her a curt nod before moving along the line to converse with the other medical members of the team. It was easier to deal with him when he was in doctor mode because it reminded her of the days when they'd been able to work together before chemistry and emotions had got in the way. If he maintained this detached manner and avoided any further mention over their shared past she was more likely to hold back the tears and the urge to slap him.

Freya stepped on board the bus with renewed fire in her belly. She'd survived the loss of her baby in her teens and had made it through this last year of absolute hell, so she knew she could get through anything.

'Look at the big snowmen!' Hope and Scarlett had their faces squished up against the bus windows, pointing at the sights along the way, and Freya had to admit she was every bit as impressed by the ten-foot-high figures greeting them on arrival at the clearing where they were to begin their activities.

They'd made a quick stop to check in at their accommodation first, leaving all unnecessary baggage except the medical equipment they needed and an estranged husband she suddenly couldn't seem to shake off, and now she was ready to go exploring.

'Isn't it wonderful?' With the falling snow, frosted pine trees and the marshmallow landscape waiting for the first footsteps to break the surface, this place was exactly what she needed to compensate for last year's miserable time.

The trio was so engrossed by their surroundings that they were last to leave the bus and found the others were already lined up, waiting for the reindeer sleighs to take them through the magical forest, when they stepped outside.

Lucas was waiting to speak to her at the back of the line. 'They can only take two at a time.'

'Well, how's that going to work for us?' The girls were clutching both of her hands and there was no way she could leave one behind or expect them to go without her.

'I've volunteered to take one of the girls with me. It's not a problem.'

Maybe not to him but as it seemed the volunteers had all been allocated already to accompany the children along with the medical staff, and she didn't want them to miss out, she had no other option than to accept his solution to the problem.

'Fine. You go on ahead with Scarlett and I'll follow with Hope.' At least the moment wouldn't be totally ruined if she wasn't expected to snuggle up beside him. Sleigh rides in the snow were supposed to be fun and romantic and definitely not something to be shared with a soon-to-be ex-husband.

In contrast, Scarlett was only too eager to climb onto the wooden frame with Lucas, and Freya was able to breathe a little easier once they'd begun their journey deep into the woods without her.

'Our turn next.' She gave Hope's hand a squeeze and exchanged cheesy grins with her as their ride arrived.

The figure leading the reindeer towards them was dressed in the bright red and blue, embroidered traditional costume of the area, adding to the wonder of it all. The reindeer was a magnificent beast, his harness the same colourful fabric of his master, and his majestic antlers dusted with snow. He was so awe-inspiring he could've stepped straight out of one of those sentimental movies her mum insisted on watching every year.

'Can I stroke him?' Hope whispered, bubbling with

delight at meeting what she probably imagined was one of Father Christmas's faithful servants.

The handler nodded and gave them the go-ahead to get the most from this experience. Freya let Hope pet his muzzle first but she didn't get in the sleigh until she'd had her chance to touch the soft brown fur herself. It was the kind of quiet, contemplative moment that gave her a pang of regret she didn't have a child of her own to share it with. She often imagined what her baby would've looked like if it had survived, but it didn't matter how much she tortured herself—she would never know. The need to be a mother again had almost consumed her when she and Lucas had married, she had been so desperate to fill that hole in her heart. This guardianship was as close as she'd get when she'd been let down one too many times by those who'd promised to be there for her.

If her first fiancé hadn't run out on her when he'd found out she was pregnant at eighteen, she might never have had the miscarriage. Although she would never know the cause for sure, the stress of having to face life as a single mother straight out of high school had been overwhelming at the time and would surely have contributed to the tragedy. It was only nursing and the thought she might still become a parent someday, with a man who actually loved her, that had got her through her grief. To have history repeat itself and her husband abandon her and that dream of motherhood had been a bereavement all over again. She was reminded of it every time she looked at him.

'Can he really fly?' Hope's excited chatter about the

reindeer was a welcome interruption to her journey into self-pity but also a further reminder of everything she'd lost and now would probably never experience. She wouldn't be part of that parent and child club that got to take part in those simple pleasures of storytelling or leaving snacks out for Santa Claus and his magical reindeer on Christmas Eve. Freya's parents had made the whole time so special for her she'd always looked forward to doing the same for her own children. As though re-creating that world of make-believe would somehow bring back the magic she'd lost along with her precious baby on that cold December night. Now, with that last hope taken from her, there seemed very little reason for her to celebrate that time of year at all.

'Only on Christmas Eve, I'm afraid, and with the help of very special fairy dust the elves add to their food.' Freya stopped herself from sliding back too far into her heartache for Hope's sake and took her seat for the big adventure. Everything seemed a lot more fun when you still believed in the magic.

The sleigh ride turned out to be a leisurely journey, and though the temperature dropped the deeper they travelled into the woods, they remained toasty warm under the warm woollen blanket covering their laps.

A sudden flash of movement through the trees caused Hope to cry out, 'Look! It's Scarlett and Dr Lucas!'

Sure enough, every now and again she caught a glimpse of the other two members of the party, grinning and waving frantically at them as they passed on the other side of the track. She couldn't help but wave back with the same enthusiasm as the others. As long as Lucas didn't read anything more into it than her joining in the fun, they'd get through this. She hadn't forgiven him anything and doubted she ever would.

When they came to the end of the trail, the others, including Lucas and his tiny new sidekick, had formed a semicircle around the staff member nominated as event coordinator and were listening intently to his instructions.

'We have a few activities on offer for you today. If you would like to start at alternate stations and make your way around it will be easier for everyone to have their turn. You will find bathroom facilities in the small building behind us along with a seating area for anyone who finds they want a break or needs to get indoors to warm up. We have storytelling in the tepee tent, there are husky sleigh rides, snowmobiles for the more adventurous among us and, of course, the cookout over the campfire where you'll be able to fill your bellies.'

'I know which one I'm looking forward to.' Lucas managed to raise a few laughs from the adults, his easygoing nature making it easy for people to like him, but Freya didn't want to be one of them. She wanted to maintain an emotional detachment from him until this trip was over and she could really let loose about how she felt.

'Let me guess—we need to go in pairs?' She cursed herself for being so slow off the bus and putting herself in this position again.

'Is that going to be a problem?' He cocked his head

to one side, the picture of innocence. Once upon a time that playfulness would've made her laugh, or swoon, but now that kind of teasing simply set her teeth on edge. They weren't friends, and they certainly weren't lovers entitled to flirt. It was deliberate goading.

'Do you want me to swap?' Gillian sidled up to her with the little boy she'd been tasked with minding clinging to her, and butted in on the conversation, her face a mask of concern.

'No, it wouldn't be fair on the kids to cause any upheaval now when we've all bonded. Honestly, it's no problem at all,' Freya reassured her friend, even though they all knew that being tied to her ex for the rest of this weekend was going to test her patience severely.

Lucas had never intended to be so actively involved when he'd assumed this role. He'd simply volunteered as a favour to his colleague with the added bonus of boosting his profile again and showing any doubters he was still the same doctor he'd been before his illness had stripped him of everything. That was before he'd discovered his ex-wife was part of the medical team.

He could easily have switched with someone else then, just as he could've swapped with one of the volunteers now, or gone on ahead and let her catch up, but he hadn't been able to resist the chance to spend some time with her again when presented with the opportunity. It was the same fascination and wanting her company he'd had when he'd first laid eyes on her and he'd made any excuse to see her inside and outside work.

It had been tough enough convincing himself he no

longer loved Freya when they'd been separated but it was nigh on impossible having seen her again. These past months he'd had his legion of demons to keep him company but now he was free, he realised how much he missed being with Freya. That notion of completely severing all ties now seemed like extra punishment rather than a new beginning.

He'd kept himself busy, trying to reclaim his life and focusing on work, but she'd been very much a part of that life and it was difficult to let go. Especially when the woman he loved wasn't even attempting to disguise her contempt for him. He couldn't blame her when to all intents and purposes he'd walked out of their marriage without a second glance. She wasn't to know he'd spent the best part of a year simply trying to survive the trauma of his past or that her determination to start a family as soon as possible had terrified him. His fear about becoming his father had robbed her of a chance at motherhood too.

It was only now, seeing that haunted expression in her eyes every time she looked at him, he realised she'd suffered as he had. She needed to enjoy this trip as much as the children and rediscover some of that innocence he'd stolen from her, and she couldn't do that when he was here, reminding her what he'd done. He wanted to make amends so she could leave all of that obvious anger and hurt behind and enjoy the rest of her life without any bitterness holding her back. If she would let him close enough to explain the reason behind his departure she might learn to forgive him, even if he'd made it impossible for her to love him again.

'So, Scarlett, where do you want to start?' His little pink-cheeked companion was waiting patiently by his side for more adventures and he wasn't about to discard his responsibilities in the pursuit of salvaging his conscience.

'Can we do that?' She pointed towards the hill of snow where the wooden toboggans were perched, waiting for passengers.

'I think we can manage that, can't we, Freya?' There was less of a queue for the more traditional idea of fun compared to the exciting husky rides and the snow-mobiles. He was glad they wouldn't have much of an audience when sledding would be a first for him too. At least it would break them all in gently before the more adventurous pursuits began.

Freya eyed the small hill, and him warily, her arched eyebrow disappearing beneath her cream woolly bobble hat. She was equally as cute in her layers of thermal outerwear as she'd been in her sexy elf costume but she was definitely still rebelling against the notion of being in close proximity to him.

'Do I have a choice?' she muttered, for his benefit alone, as the girls ran ahead as fast as their little legs could wade through the deep snow.

'Always.' He might want her to give him the time of day but he wouldn't force her to be with him if the idea was so distasteful.

'Really?' She didn't have to say any more than that for him to realise he hadn't actually given her a choice when it came to ending their marriage but she didn't wait for him to apologise for it. He knew her reluctance was nothing to do with the activity and everything to do with him but apparently she'd decided to see this through regardless of his presence since she was off, trudging up the hill behind the girls.

Once they were all at the top of the hill they separated into pairs again, having deemed it safer for them to accompany the girls rather than let them sled on their own. The air was colder up here and even the inside of his nose felt as though it was beginning to freeze. He didn't want the girls exposed to the elements any more than necessary.

'How about a race?' It seemed a straightforward run down the hill, no obstacles, trees or dips to worry about, so even the most inexperienced riders could manage the route with relative ease.

'Yay!' Scarlett and Hope were jumping up and down so vigorously he had to quieten them down again in case the excitement became too much for either of them.

Freya didn't fight him on this one, probably because her nose was getting redder by the second too and this was the quickest way back down the hill. They took the reins in their respective toboggans with the girls tucked securely in front and the bags containing their medication stowed safely with them.

'On your marks…'

'Get set…'

'Go!' the four of them chorused as they tipped over the brow of the hill.

The wind whipped at his face as they sped into the snowy abyss but he barely noticed, lost in the exhilaration of it all and being that carefree kid he'd never been before. The shrieks of laughter around him only added to the enjoyment, with even the sound of his own echoing back at him from the forest.

He couldn't say which of them finished first because for him it had become more about that sense of pure freedom of speeding down the hill rather than the race itself.

'That was amazing!' There was a moment when Freya was actually smiling at him as they came to rest, her face glowing with excitement in a brief unguarded moment, making him yearn for more. It brought back memories of their early dates, having fun together when they hadn't had a care in the world. He wanted her to look at him the way she used to, without that constant suspicion.

'It reminds me of the time we did that obstacle race for charity. Do you remember? We slid the whole way to the bottom of the hill in the pouring rain.' They'd laughed the whole way down and Freya's gung-ho attitude to the whole course had impressed him. He'd fallen in love with her that day as she'd tackled rope ladders and crawled under tarpaulins with a grin on her face and dirt in her hair. Her *joie de vivre* had been irresistible and he'd known then he didn't want to be without her. He still didn't.

'I've never seen so much mud in my life.' Her sweet laugh was almost as much of a surprise now as it had been then. Even though she'd been covered from head to toe she'd found only humour in the situation, which had made her utterly adorable.

'And they wouldn't let us on the bus back until we'd been hosed down.' There was another part to that story that wasn't suitable for present company but he saw the rush of blood to her cheeks and knew she was also thinking of the steamy shower they'd taken together later at his place afterwards.

'At least we'll stay nice and dry today.' She got out of the toboggan and dusted down her clothes, the moment over.

'I can't believe we've never done that before.' He helped the girls back to their feet, wondering how different things could've been between him and Freya. There was a reason they'd never gone sledding or done any of this fun festive stuff together. He'd been too caught up in his past to make new, more pleasant memories associated with the season. If anything, he'd gone on to make matters worse. He'd left her at Christmas and he could see the very second she remembered it too as she turned away from him, back towards their two charges, who were tossing handfuls of ploughed snow at each other.

'Hands up who wants to go get some hot chocolate.'

'Me!' Gloves and voices shot up into the air at once, including Lucas's. He could do with a little warmth when the atmosphere between the adults was becoming frostier by the second.

They trekked back towards the others, where he did a quick check to make sure the activity hadn't had any impact on Hope's blood-sugar level before they had their warm drinks and hot dogs. He was making a note of everything she ate and drank today so they could adjust her insulin accordingly later.

Once he'd had his fill, Lucas left them keeping warm by the fire so he could check on the others. When he was satisfied there were no medical emergencies and everyone else was enjoying their day, he made it back in time for toasting marshmallows over the fire.

'Here, you can help.' Freya handed him two of the wooden sticks with marshmallows skewered on the end. Even though he knew it was to save the girls from getting their hands too close to the open fire, he wanted to see it as a truce of sorts where she no longer saw him as the enemy.

'How do you know when they're done?' he asked, holding the sticks tentatively over the fire as the heat seared through his gloves.

When there was no answer forthcoming, he looked up to see Freya tilt her head to one side, amusement dancing with the reflection of the flickering flames in her eyes. 'Are you serious?'

'I just want to make sure I get it right for the girls,' he said with a huff.

This was beyond the realms of his usual out-of-hours leisure pursuits, not that he had many these days. Sledding or toasting marshmallows hadn't been part of his childhood reality or on any syllabus when he'd had his head buried in medical books to escape the horrors of it. He certainly hadn't much call, or want, to do it since.

'You just want a light golden colour. Don't let it burn and make sure they're cooled down enough before you try to eat them.' She stopped teasing and seemed to thaw a little towards him as she coaxed him through the basic skills of marshmallow toasting.

Perhaps it was her caring nature that made her willing to help him out but he wanted to believe it was because she could see he was still the old Lucas at heart. The one who'd never meant to hurt her. The one she used to love. He longed for them both to break free from the memory of that broken man he'd become at the end of their marriage.

'These are really good.' Along with the others he tucked into the gooey white molten goodness with gusto and did his best to lick off the sticky sweetness coating his lips so he didn't waste a morsel or a second of this experience. This could be the last time she let him this close to her again.

'You missed a bit.' She pulled off her mitten and brushed the corner of his mouth with the soft pad of her thumb.

It was an innocent gesture but the moment she touched him his whole body sparked to life, every nerve ending tingling with awareness. As though he'd been dormant for too long, a soulless creature waiting for her to initiate that contact, that bolt of electricity, to awaken him from his slumber.

'Thanks.' He locked his eyes on hers and he saw a brief flare of desire before she blinked it away. They might only have been married a short while but he knew his wife well enough to recognise that look. It was the same flicker of interest he'd found so hard to resist when they'd first started working together and he still didn't want to. He could see that same internal fight against it in her eyes too and hope flared in his chest along with desire.

The most he thought he could ask from her was forgiveness so he could start his new life over, never imagining the one good thing from his past might still be available to him. He'd simply accepted that he'd hurt her too much to ever go back. If she did still harbour feelings for him somewhere beyond that tough shell she'd cocooned herself in, it conflicted more than ever with his original plan for a permanent split. It brought them straight back to square one, where he knew walking away was best for her but when the time came would inflict more suffering on them both.

'They're very messy girls, aren't they?' She fussed around the girls, wiping their mouths and hands in what he figured was an attempt to undermine the significance of the moment they'd had. It didn't work when he could see how flustered she was and she could barely look in his direction. She'd never been very good at disguising her feelings for him, which was what had made him break his rule about dating work colleagues in the first place.

'We'll have to do that again over the weekend.' He wasn't just talking about the sweet treat. If they went back to Scotland without resolving what had happened they'd both be doomed to wallow in their misery for the rest of their days. They needed another moment together; a chance to reconnect properly where he could make amends and finally give them the closure they needed.

* * *

'I doubt we'll find the time.' Freya didn't know if he meant toasting marshmallows, talking about their early days together, or another brief moment when she forgot everything except how much she wished they were still together, but all of those scenarios were too dangerous to repeat.

When he was joining in with the kids, doing things he'd apparently never done before, it was too easy to forget they'd been apart for so long. The sight of him so youthful, so carefree took her back to the time when they'd enjoyed each other's company to the exclusion of everything else. It was painful to watch at times when she was no closer to understanding what had brought the sudden change in him and turned him into the distant man who'd eventually walked out on her.

Perhaps she should've confronted him the second she'd heard about his reappearance back into society but she'd worried it might just tip her over the edge of sanity. She'd barely held it together after realising he wasn't coming back to her but she'd also been afraid the sight of him again would prove too painful, that her feelings for him would remain the same despite what he'd done. She'd been afraid of this.

It was vital for her well-being to focus on everything his betrayal had cost her—her marriage, her trust and her chance of baby-filled happiness—instead of attraction and naivety, which had blinded her to danger too often. The only thing she needed from him was a reason for destroying the life she'd planned for them, and nothing more.

She moved the girls on towards the storyteller in the tent so they were safely back in company. With his wooden staff and flowing purple robes he could've been some mystical shaman from the Middle Ages, but the girls were more fascinated than afraid. They edged ever closer to listen to his Christmas tales, leaving the adults in the cold, and she could see Lucas glancing back at the campfire, and most likely the marshmallows, with longing.

'Have you honestly never done any of this sort of thing before? Not even at school?' Freya couldn't quite get her head around the notion a grown man hadn't experienced any of these basic pleasures in life. She knew he'd struggled with her idea of fun at Christmas but he'd never opened up to tell her why. Every time she'd tried to ask him what it was that troubled him so much about it, he'd shut down the conversation and pushed her away. Until living under the same roof had become unbearable.

'Nope.' He still wasn't giving anything away and made her want to shake the information out of him. She'd only ever wanted to understand him and it hurt that he'd never been able to trust her with the sort of personal information a wife should've known—the history of ex-loves and family and all of those experiences that formed a person.

Of course, she hadn't been able to share some important events in her own life but that was because she'd tried to bury them in order to create a future with him. Lucas had given little information about himself and she wasn't convinced it had been in order to benefit their relationship.

Looking back, anytime she'd enquired about his life pre-medical school he'd always distracted her with a kiss, or more. Infatuated as she had been, she had always given in to temptation instead of pushing the subject. Later, towards the end of their relationship, he hadn't bothered to employ any such tactics and had simply refused to answer any questions, that ever-present scowl declaring the matter off limits.

It rankled now that she'd been too blinded by love to see the obvious flaws in their marriage when he'd insisted on erecting that barrier. She'd been so desperate to create the perfect family she'd ignored the first signs of discord and had ploughed ahead with her obsession for a child at all costs. Her blinkered naivety and his insular behaviour had ensured they would never have succeeded as a couple. Yet, even though he was still refusing to be drawn on his personal history, there was something different about him. That willingness to participate in activities beyond his comfort zone had been distinctly lacking during their last time together and her temper was rising at the injustice of it all.

'So what's changed?' Her blunt questioning was directly in line with her sudden desire to uncover the facts. This new Lucas was embracing all the clichés he'd professed to despise when they'd been together and she'd been the one to bear the brunt of his dark moods because of it. It was only natural she should want to know who, or what, had brought about this new attitude. Even if the thought of someone taking her place, sharing a deeper bond with her husband than she apparently had, made her want to weep. At the time she would've done anything to save her marriage, if only she'd been given the chance.

'I came here for the kids. Every child deserves at least one happy time in their lives to look back on.' As a round of applause sounded for the storyteller Lucas bent down to receive a running hug from the returning Scarlett and Hope. There was such a haunted expression on his face it reached that mothering instinct deep inside her and she had to catch the sob in her throat before she embarrassed them all.

It occurred to her then that his own upbringing remained somewhat of a mystery to her. His mother had left home when he was very little, and he had no siblings—he'd revealed that much in the early days, when they'd been getting to know each other—but when it had come to mention of his father, he'd changed the subject, or distracted her, every time. When Lucas had refused to even invite him to their wedding she'd just assumed it had been a strained relationship. Watching him interact with the children now and replaying his words made her question what kind of childhood he'd actually had.

It was a sobering thought to realise she'd never really known who her husband was beyond the man he'd become. Even more so to discover she still wanted to find out.

CHAPTER THREE

FREYA WAS NUMB and not just from the wind and ice sprayed in her face after they'd travelled the snowy plains at high speed on the snowmobiles. Her smile was frozen on for the girls' sakes, but though she was saying and doing all the right things so they didn't know anything was amiss, her head and heart were scrambled, trying to come to terms with a very different Lucas from the last one she'd seen.

He certainly seemed keen to remind her about the good times they'd had together, sending her emotions into a dizzying jumble as she tried to protect herself by recalling those agonising last days of their marriage. When he was smiling at her or playing with the children it was easy to forget they were no longer together. Unless he'd had that chip on his shoulder surgically removed she didn't know what had caused the change in him, which made his past behaviour seem even more erratic in comparison. Despite the nights she'd spent cursing the man's name she found herself clinging to the hope there was something behind it other than being single again. If she had more information to explain the state of his mind then and now she might be able to look back on these past months in a completely different light.

There'd been that one moment when he'd opened the door to his past and let her have the briefest glimpse inside. Unfortunately, she'd been shut out from gathering any more info of a personal nature once he'd thrown himself back into his role of medical supervisor and children's entertainer as they'd continued their day of adventure.

'What did you think was the most fun today?' he asked everybody as they piled on the bus at the end of the day.

'The huskies.'

'Tobogganing.'

'Building snowmen.'

Everyone clearly had their own favourite activity of the day but they all had that same joyful expression as they animatedly swapped stories of their adventures. Apart from Scarlett, who was asleep on Lucas's shoulder, and Hope, who was gently snoring in the seat next to Freya. Exhaustion had finally claimed them. She didn't know if he was using the sleeping child as some sort of buffer to keep her away as he made his way down the stationary bus to his seat but he didn't appear to be in a hurry to discard the little girl dribbling over his shoulder. He'd always had a special rapport with the kids he treated. He was very comfortable in their company and never, ever talked down to them. It was one of the many reasons patients and families loved him and one of the reasons she'd known he would've made a wonderful father.

'What about you, Dr Lucas? What was your favourite thing?' One of the children turned the question back on him and Freya watched and listened for the reply as intently as the tiny interviewer.

She hadn't managed to coax him into enjoying any of the family Christmas traditions she'd been so keen to uphold but she'd seen a whole new side to him today. He'd really thrown himself into the part of Santa's little helper but she couldn't help but wonder if it had been solely for the children's benefit. After all, he'd proved to be a good actor before when she'd believed they had been happily married, only to have him leave her at the worst possible time of the year.

'Um… I have to say it was toasting marshmallows over the fire.' He caught her eye for a split second and the heat of that moment warmed her chilled bones as she recalled that moment when she'd touched him again.

A few days ago, if someone had told her she'd meet up with her ex-husband the only physical contact she would've imagined making had been a swift kick somewhere delicate as payback for the hurt he'd caused her. Not tenderly brushing melted marshmallow from his lips as though they were still together with that spark between them very much alive. She didn't enjoy that hitch in her breath as they connected over the heads of the children filing past because it drew attention to those lingering feelings she apparently still had for him. After everything he'd done and the time they'd had apart, he shouldn't be able to have any effect on her other than the need to hate him. More than that, it left her open for more pain from someone who clearly hadn't loved her enough to stay with her.

Curiosity and a need to salve her own conscience over the end of their marriage might be pushing her towards him for more answers but she'd have to remain wary of getting too close. She wouldn't survive falling for him a second time.

Roll on tomorrow when they were on a plane back to reality and their now very separate lives.

The duo of snow-dusted log cabins welcoming them home for the night was a Christmas card come to life. The orange glow spilling out from the windows into the dark night definitely made Freya want to kick off her boots at the door and take a place by the fireplace inside. Which was exactly what she would do when the children had been fed, the necessary medication administered and everyone readied for bed.

'Thank goodness they got caterers in. That's all I can say.' Freya handed the last plate to Lucas to dry and drained the soapy water out of the sink.

'I know. I'm shattered.' Gillian opened the cupboards to put away the now clean dishes as their efficient production line rid all traces of the group dinner. The hot buffet provided by the hotel to the larger cabin on their return had saved them a lot of extra work but the trio had volunteered for washing-up duty once everyone had taken their fill.

'There wasn't much left over, which means we

don't have to worry about any picky eaters not getting enough nutrition. I think everyone worked up quite an appetite out there today.' Lucas folded the tea towel and set it neatly on the counter. He'd always been tidy and not one of those men who insisted on leaving wet towels on the floor or a general trail of mess behind him. With more than a hint of sadness Freya realised he'd never expected her to pick up after him as though she were some sort of replacement parent, had never needed her to look after him. The single life probably suited him better than marriage.

'Now we just have to entertain them for a while until they're finally worn out,' Gillian said with the waning enthusiasm of someone whose energy had deserted her before the evening programme.

'There are a stack of board games for those who want to play, and I have a Christmas CD for a good old sing-along before bed.' It was coming to that time of the evening when they were going to split into their gender-specific groups for bedtime and, tired though she was, Freya wasn't ready for the day to be over. There'd been a truce of sorts between her and Lucas but she couldn't promise tomorrow would be the same once she'd had the night to dwell on events.

'I brought some things that might help pass the time too.' Lucas cleared his throat, and though it wasn't a surprise he'd be opposed to the singing idea, she and Gillian were stunned into silence with the idea he'd come up with an alternative.

'If you can get everybody assembled around the table, I'll pop over to the other cabin to grab my supplies.'

Without giving them a chance to quiz him about what exactly he had in mind, he disappeared into the night and left them no choice but to follow his instruction.

As they gathered the group together, Freya had some reservations about whether or not he was going to deliver something to match the kids' excitement. Or if he would even come back at all. Her residual trust issues were sufficient that she was only able to relax when he kept his word and did eventually return, carrying supplies.

'Arts and crafts?' she enquired as he unloaded packages onto the table.

'A little something I made earlier.' He looked so pleased with himself it was impossible not to trust he might have something pretty cool up his sleeve after all.

'Gingerbread men?' Gillian was the first to inspect the pre-cut cardboard shapes, her discovery drawing Freya's attention sharply.

'I thought we could have some fun decorating them.' Sure enough, he provided glue sticks and coloured felt pens to everyone waiting eagerly around the table. Bright buttons and tubes of glitter soon followed, along with a selection of googly eyes to add some personality to the 2D characters.

'What a great idea.' Such a great idea, Gillian was soon abandoning Freya to get stuck in herself.

'It really was very thoughtful of you.' She had to acknowledge what he'd done when there was so much meaning to her personally behind the ordinarily simple gesture.

Not only did this signify he'd thought ahead for the children, disproving her earlier theory that this change in him could be an act, but perhaps also showing an attempt to make up for snubbing the activity last Christmas. He would've known how much this one small act of kindness would mean to her and damn it if the sight of naked gingerbread men and buttons didn't bring a tear to her eye.

'I know it's not the same as decorating freshly baked gingerbread but I thought this was something we could all enjoy instead of leaving out anyone with special dietary requirements. I'm sorry you missed out last year.' He left her in no doubt that he'd been thinking about her as much as the children before going to lend a helping hand to those who couldn't quite manage on their own.

Freya was mesmerised by the picture of him in the middle of the children, concentrating on producing a smiling symbol of everything he'd once despised. It was both heart-warming and heartbreaking to watch when it was all she'd ever wanted for him as much as for herself. They might've been doing this with children of their own if they'd stuck things out a little longer, but they would never know for sure and it certainly wouldn't help her sanity to keep imagining the family that didn't exist.

Lucas glanced up and caught her watching him, but instead of looking away, embarrassed by the attention, he held her gaze and offered a poignant half-smile in return. The regret over what they'd lost was there in his sad blue eyes as much as it was in her flip-flopping stomach. Perhaps if they'd worked harder on their marriage they could've eventually found this level of contentment together.

'Can I have a drink? I'm really thirsty.' Hope tugged on Freya's jumper and helped break the meaningful eye contact that was already putting her in danger of falling for Lucas's charm offensive a second time.

One day back in his company and she was already in turmoil. Another twenty-four hours and she dreaded to think what more havoc he might wreak on her bewildered heart.

'Sure. Have you finished colouring?' Freya ushered the more deserving cause for her attention towards the kitchen area to pour her a glass of water.

'Uh-huh. I'm going to take it home for my mummy. I don't feel well.'

Freya knelt down to take a closer look at the little girl. 'You are a little pale. We should go and check your blood sugar, sweetheart, just to make sure you're okay.'

'I want to go to bed,' Hope whined, at the prospect of the finger-prick test, but it really was important they check her levels before they let her sleep.

It had been a long day and there was always a risk of hyperglycaemia with the increased physical activity and change in routine for her. If left untreated, high blood sugar could lead to a medical emergency—ketoacidosis, a lack of insulin, or dehydration. Her sudden thirst and tiredness were symptoms Freya would not take a risk of ignoring.

'I know, and you will, as soon as we do a quick test.' She took Hope's hand and ushered her towards the door, stopping briefly to have a quiet word with Lucas on the way.

'Could you please keep Hope's gingerbread man safe for her? She's feeling quite thirsty all of a sudden, and tired.' There was no need to panic the others but it was enough information to galvanise the medical lead on this trip.

As she led Hope towards the dorm she could hear Lucas making arrangements for someone else to watch over Scarlett and making his excuses to leave.

Freya helped Hope get ready for bed, made sure her hands were clean and the BM machine was calibrated before she attempted to draw a sample of blood.

'I'm just going to check your blood-sugar level to calculate how much insulin I might need to give you to make sure you feel better. This will be all over in a second.' Even though she went through this every day, it was important Freya reminded her whimpering patient what she was doing and why they were doing it as she pricked her finger.

'You are such a brave girl. I'm sure Father Christmas is going to have a special present for you tomorrow.'

Freya squeezed the tip of her finger until there was enough blood to drip onto the testing strip.

'Are you done yet?' Hope squirmed on the bed next to her as Freya inserted the test strip into the handheld device for analysis.

'Almost. I just need you to hold this on your finger for me.' Freya pressed a cotton ball onto the skin to prevent further bleeding while she disposed of the lancet into the sharps bin.

Unfortunately, the results were, as she suspected, high enough to give cause for concern.

'Knock. Knock.' Lucas gave a courtesy tap on the door before he walked in anyway.

'Hey.' Freya handed him the blood analysis and shifted on the bed to make room for him. After all, he was the doctor in charge and not merely the man she was afraid of being too close to again.

She saw the clench of his teeth with the unfavourable result but he quickly resumed his perfect bedside manner for the little girl trying to burrow down under her bed sheets.

'I know you're tired and out of sorts, Hope, but you know we only want to keep you safe. Right?'

She nodded solemnly.

'Good girl. We can't let you sleep just yet but... I did bring a very special book to read to you before bedtime.' He produced a colourful, sparkly hardboard book from his medical bag, along with her notes and her insulin.

Freya tried to sneak a glance at the title—something about a very forgetful elf—as she tidied away Hope's discarded clothes and tried to suppress a grin. He really had planned ahead.

She folded the small pair of waterproof trousers over her arm, only for a torrent of half-eaten food and sweet wrappers to fall from the pockets onto the floor.

'What on earth—?'

Both adults stared at the evidence of a serious food

binge before turning to the tiny culprit currently hugging her knees on the bed.

'Hope? Did you eat all this extra food when we weren't looking?' Lucas kept his voice soft enough not to spook Hope any further while Freya collected the remnants of Hope's ill-gotten gains from the floor. Some of the food had obviously been pocketed from the buffet at dinner but the chocolate-bar wrappers looked suspiciously like the ones she'd seen some of the other children with earlier.

Hope hugged her knees tighter and hid her face with her hair.

'You're not in trouble. We just need to know if that's what's making your poorly.' Freya threw the rubbish in the bin. She'd take it with her to dispose of later so as not to leave further temptation behind.

There was an almost imperceptible nod and Freya brushed the child's hair from her eyes so they could see her properly. Hope nodded again.

'Thank you for telling us. It's very important we know what you've eaten today so we can work out what medicine to give you.' Lucas remained very calm, even though he must've been as concerned as Freya to discover the extra food consumption, which meant they would have to adjust the dose of insulin to be administered. By not overreacting to this slip-up, it prevented Hope from getting further stressed, which wouldn't have helped matters.

They were going to be in for a long night of monitoring her condition to make sure no medical emergency arose as a result of her little rebellion. It was only natural a child would want to help themselves to sweets and treats they weren't usually allowed but in Hope's case it could cause much more than a stomach ache. They had to point out the importance of sticking to the rules without scaring her too much.

Lecture over, Lucas afforded Freya another moment of his attention. 'I can stay here with Hope through the night if you'd like. I'll give her her insulin and I'm happy to pull up a chair for the night if you want to see to Scarlett. We have a book to read anyway, don't we, Hope?' Lucas distracted Hope away from the night ahead of blood tests and injections with the shiny promise of his one-to-one attention. He'd honed that diversionary skill to perfection but at least he was using it for the greater good on this occasion.

'Are you sure?' She knew they couldn't both stay here when they had the responsibility of Scarlett's condition and medication to supervise too, but she hadn't expected such a display of magnanimity from him.

'Of course. You get some sleep and I'll see you in the morning.'

Freya stepped out of the bedroom and took a deep, shaky breath to recover some of the composure she was threatening to lose as he started reading to his captivated audience. This warm, caring side of him was exactly why she'd fallen in love with him. It was lovely to see this grown man relaxed and giving his time to comfort a child, but it also made her wonder why he hadn't been able to extend that compassion to her for the duration of their marriage.

* * *

Freya woke early and, after checking on the girls, made her way into the kitchen to make a cup of coffee. She'd been so physically and mentally drained she'd fallen asleep in her clothes but it hadn't been a peaceful slumber by any means. Her thoughts had been with her husband in the other room; dreams of the perfect Christmas they should've had together and memories of the painful reality. Most disturbing of all had been the erotic nature their reunion had taken in her subconscious until she'd woken, breathless and a tad frustrated. At least she'd managed to resist tucking a blanket around him as an excuse to touch the real version when she'd peeked into the room and found him sleeping in one of the hard kitchen chairs.

She poured herself a strong shot of caffeine and carried it into the lounge area. It was still dark outside but she was comforted by the sound of the fire still crackling in the hearth. Without the trappings of modern life out here in the wilds and the constant hum of technology around her there was a peacefulness she'd usually welcome before the start of what could prove to be another long day. She pulled the warm wool blanket off the sofa and tucked it around her feet, sipped her drink and watched the flames flicker in the fireplace but she just couldn't seem to relax. It was only when Lucas walked into the room that she realised it was because she'd been on tenterhooks, waiting to see him again.

This was more than anxiety creeping through her body at the prospect of finally finding out what had prompted their separation in the first place. She found she was actually looking forward to being in his company again. Regardless of how things had ended between them, switching her feelings off for him hadn't been as straightforward as she'd imagined.

Even now her pulse fluttered as he walked into the living room the same way it used to when they'd crossed paths at work. When she had been unable to help the attraction to him but had known it was trouble waiting to happen. Some things never changed.

There was a moment as he walked into the open-plan dining room/living room when he seemed to be looking for someone, or something. Vanity and that unwavering ache in her heart wanted it to be her.

'Oh…er…hi. You're up early.' He did a double take as he spotted her on the sofa and his relaxed smile when he saw her appeared to prove her fancy correct.

'Sorry—did I wake you? I was trying to be quiet.'

'Not at all. I smelt the coffee.' He sniffed the air, hot on the scent of his same beverage of choice.

'There's plenty in the pot.' She pointed him in the right direction while she took a moment to appreciate his rumpled clothes and tousled hair. It was doubtful he'd had any more of a restful sleep than she had but he looked good on it. *Damn him.*

'How's Scarlett?' He came to sit with her and it took a second for the implication of that to sink in. They were going to spend more enforced time together, alone and uninterrupted. As much as they probably needed to, the prospect made her wish she'd had a nip of whisky in her coffee to fortify her for the inevitable rehashing of events.

'She was fast asleep in seconds. No problems at all.' It was the truth, even if she felt a little guilty about probably having an easier night than he'd had.

'Good. Good. Hope's last blood-sugar check was normal, so she was able to get some rest in the end too.'

Now that they'd established both of their patients were healthy and safe, tense anticipation seemed to fill the sudden conversational void between them. There was never going to be a better opportunity for them this weekend to work out their issues in private, if either of them were ready for it.

Although if his apparent disregard for her feelings had remained unchanged from their last days together, she doubted he'd have come down and risked spending time alone with her. He knew her well enough to know she'd want answers now more than ever.

As torturous as this would be, she needed to understand the reasons behind the failure of the relationship so she could either learn from her mistakes or point the finger of blame somewhere other than at the mirror. There was no point in letting this fester and spoil another Christmas for both of them.

Any other man probably should've been cringing at the idea of having an in-depth conversation with his ex about what had led to their break-up. Not least because of her initial, understandable reaction to seeing him on the plane for the first time. Instead, Lucas had found himself restlessly wishing the night away so he could finally clear the air with Freya.

He knew they'd had a breakthrough in their frosty

relationship with her apparent acceptance of his apology and their prolonged eye contact over his craft project. Hope suddenly taking ill had been the much-needed antidote to letting Freya get too far into his system again, though he'd have preferred a less stressful alternative for all of their sakes. Now they were alone together there was so much he needed to say to her, he didn't know where to begin.

He drained his still-hot coffee, taking the top layer of skin from the roof of his mouth, and walked over to rinse his cup in the sink, stalling for time in the hope appropriate words would somehow form in his mouth during the short trip back to his seat.

'They did a good job with the decorations, didn't they?' He flicked one of the silver baubles carefully hung on the tree in the corner of the room.

Freya nodded. 'It looks lovely. Very well-coordinated.'

She was being very diplomatic in the face of his epic procrastination. He knew her taste ran more towards colourful and as gaudy as possible. The twinkling white fairy lights and fragile decorations strung around the real Christmas tree were very pretty but a far cry from her eclectic collection of tat, which leaned more towards sentimentality than any aesthetic purpose. He'd heard her call this kind of sparse display as cold and clinical before and it wouldn't fit in with her penchant for chubby sugar plum fairies and handmade ornaments she hoarded from local craft fairs.

'I imagine it's a dream come true for you too, being in the midst of all this.' He gestured towards the garlands and stockings adorning the fireplace, which were more homely and in keeping with her style of storybook decor.

She shrugged her shoulders. 'Once upon a time it would've been. I'm finding it doesn't quite hold the same appeal for me any more.'

There was no need for her to point the finger of blame at him for that; the weight of guilt was already crushing him at the apathy she'd apparently developed towards the season. The disease that was his father had claimed another victim and he was sick to the stomach he'd been an accessory to the murder of her Christmas spirit.

'I'm sorry to hear that. You were always so...involved.' He'd never intended to take that childlike enthusiasm away from her. She'd always been so full of life, full of fun, he'd never imagined he would've been capable of draining that out of her. There were a lot of things he hadn't thought through properly during that period, his mind so twisted with rage and grief. It was only now that black cloud had dissipated he was starting to see things more clearly and realise what he'd lost in the process.

'I know you hated all of the fuss. Well, you'll be pleased to know I've cut back considerably on my tinsel addiction since then.' She made an attempt at humour but Lucas didn't find anything remotely funny in what she was telling him. It had irritated him when he'd been expected to live in Santa's grotto day after day for an entire month but that didn't mean he was happy to find he might have made her as cynical as he was about the season.

'I guess I just didn't understand it. We didn't really go in for the whole magical fairy-tale scene in our house.' That almost made him snort out loud at the thought of his inebriated father thinking of anything other than his next drink. There had been no stockings hung by the fire or milk and cookies left out for Santa. He'd been lucky if there had been any food in the house at all. It was difficult to get caught up in the wonder of it all as an adult when he hadn't experienced it as a child.

'That's a shame. Some of my best childhood memories are of Christmas, even if recent ones have proved more painful.' She left him in no doubt he was the reason she didn't feel like celebrating any more. It hadn't been a calculated move and it was typical that his father had managed to cause maximum damage with optimum timing.

'I never meant to hurt you. I just—'

'Couldn't do it any more? You said. It didn't make it any easier for me, though. I couldn't eat, couldn't sleep. I couldn't even tell my parents you'd left me for the longest time. I didn't know for sure that's what had happened until I'd exhausted all other possibilities and I got word you'd taken leave from the hospital. You didn't even take your clothes. They're still hanging in the wardrobe. Were you that desperate to get away from me, Lucas?' It was the little hiccup catching his name that finally smashed through his defences and forced him to face up to what he'd done.

'It wasn't like that, Freya.' It was all he could offer to soothe her from a distance without ripping his chest open and letting the trapped crows of his personal anguish beat their wings in flight.

'I suppose it's done now. A broken heart can't ever be truly mended, can it? Slapped back together and held together with sticky tape maybe, so a person can keep on living even though there are days she doesn't want to, but not *fixed*.'

He could hear the irreparable damage he'd left in his wake in her clipped words. Perhaps he wasn't so different from his father after all. In an attempt to avoid becoming a clone of the man who'd ruined his life by walking away, he'd done the complete opposite. He could hear that pain reflected in every word and hitch in her breath and he didn't want to burden her with any more misery than he already had.

'I honestly thought you'd be better off without me.'

'Why? What did I do to make you think that? Where did you go? Why didn't you let me know you weren't dead?' She launched a volley of questions at him that she'd probably been saving for months.

He couldn't answer any of them without making things worse and adding more to his guilt quota. It had never occurred to him that she might've believed him dead, only that he'd failed her. 'I went to Peter's—'

'Peter? Your best man? The guy who swore he didn't know where you were when I was sobbing down the phone?' She wasn't the only one he'd ticked off with that stunt. Peter hadn't spoken to him the rest of the day after that one.

'I made him lie to you. I needed space.' He tried to picture those early days, which had passed in a blur when he'd never made it out of bed, never said a word, yet Peter had insisted on bringing him food and water and keeping him in the land of the living.

The heart-wrenching gasp he pulled from her chest told of the devastation he'd caused by not letting that person be her, but he hadn't wanted her to see that image of him curled up in the foetal position, weeping like a babe.

'"In sickness and in health. Till death do us part." We made the vows, Lucas. I, for one, intended to keep them.' She was scolding him, yet she was so sincere he wanted to believe it would've been enough to get through it together. For the first time in his life, when he'd really needed someone to lean on, he'd had someone who would love him unconditionally and give him everything he'd ever wanted, pride had muscled its way in and robbed him of the gift. He'd been blind to that fact until she'd come back into his life and made him see what he was missing.

'I did too, at the time, but things change.'

'What things?' Freya threw up her hands and he knew that given half a chance she would have them around his throat. The only reason he was being so obtuse was the same one he'd used when he'd left her—to save her from the darkness that had claimed him. The least he could give her was the reassurance she'd in no way been at fault.

'Me. You know I wasn't the same man you met. Maybe I just wasn't cut out for marriage but that honestly wasn't a reflection of you. You've got a lot of Christmases ahead of you. Don't let what happened between us spoil them all for you.' He didn't want the legacy to continue. Someday she would have a family of her own and he didn't want to be responsible for ruining anyone else's childhood. That was exactly why he'd left their marriage when he'd been at his lowest point and had needed his wife more than ever. She'd deserved someone who wouldn't taint her rosy view of the world.

'I'm trying.' She made a mocking toast with her coffee before gulping it down as though it really had the special powers she'd always claimed.

It was a shame his word wasn't enough for her any more but that was his own fault. He wouldn't be able to give her an adequate explanation without digging deep into his past, so he could only hope a strong woman like Freya wouldn't have her spirits dampened for long. Unlike him, she didn't tend to dwell on the negative aspects of life. At least, she hadn't in the past. A year apart had already changed her so much he wasn't sure he knew anything about her any more.

'What was the whole deal with the over-the-top festivities anyway? I've never seen anyone tinsel-bomb a house the way you did. I don't think there was an inch of that house devoid of glitter.' A month of cheesy festive tunes and barely being able to see the football on the TV because of the stuffed woodland animals strategically placed around it had bugged him no end. However, he couldn't imagine the house in December without all the palaver. It was simply one of her quirks, which anyone other than a miserable Grinch like him would've found adorable.

She took on that faraway look in her eyes she'd always had when it had come to her favourite time of the year and he was pleased that his Mrs Christmas Fairy, as he'd nicknamed her, hadn't totally lost her mojo.

'No matter how tough things were financially, Mum and Dad always made such a big deal of it. I don't ever remember feeling as though I was missing out because it was just such a warm, cosy feeling of us being together as a family. Sorry—you probably don't want to hear that.' She shook away that glimpse of the old Freya and replaced it with the jaded wife she'd become during his absence who was afraid to express her enjoyment of it all.

Had he really been the dark cloud hovering over the holidays? He thought back to that Christmas together, when he'd frowned at her whimsy. Yes, he'd virtually beaten her into submission with his cynicism and that guilt wasn't going to be easy to live with any more than being the victim of someone else's rage.

'I wouldn't ever want to take that away from you. You're very lucky to have had such a wonderful family.' If he'd had a mum who'd stuck around or a father capable of loving his son, he knew he'd have an entirely different take on the subject. As it was, the only feelings he connected with any supposed family celebrations were ones of disappointment and fear. Not only had the needs and wishes of a little boy been frequently ignored in favour of the demon drink but it had inevitably led to an outburst of violent temper.

'You never told me anything about your father.'
Freya pulled the heavy woollen blanket up towards her
chin, cocooning herself in comfort, and he wondered if
that was what Christmas had become for her—a comfort blanket she could wrap herself up in once a year.
And he'd whipped it away, leaving her exposed to the
harsh elements of reality. He sighed and nodded, re-
signed to the fact he'd have to go some way to sharing
the gory details of his past if it would help her understand his actions and rediscover her joy.

'He wasn't worth talking about.' Lucas shrugged,
wishing he had been able to dismiss all thoughts of
him as easily as he made out. The reason he'd never
wanted to discuss his father was because talking meant
remembering and that hurt too damn much. He'd spent
his adult life trying to block out all thoughts of that
time. That hadn't worked out very well for him in the
end when the suppressed emotions had all spectacu-
larly erupted at once.

'*Wasn't?*' She picked up on that minute detail
straight away.

In the time-honoured tradition of denial he could've
pretended it was a slip of the tongue. It was even less
of her business now that they were no longer together.
Except if he ever hoped to start building bridges with
Freya he knew it had to start with the truth. At least,
as much of it he was comfortable sharing with her.

'He died. Last year. Just before Christmas.'

Lucas watched her facial expressions as she ran the
gamut of emotions that information brought to the sur-

face—shock, horror, sympathy, and finally the realisation of what that timing meant.

Suddenly he couldn't bear to watch any more. He
didn't want to confront this here and now where they
were doing their best to make childhood dreams come
true, not relive old nightmares. This unburdening of
his soul wasn't as liberating as he'd imagined when he
could feel her gaze burrowing into his skin, willing
him to give more of himself.

'You should have told me,' Freya said softly, reaching across to rest her hand on his knee, but that sympathy was exactly what he hadn't wanted from her. He'd
no wish to see pity in her eyes every time she looked at
him. He wanted her to see him as the strong man he'd
been when they'd met and not the shell he'd become
as a result of his father's reign of tyranny.

'It wouldn't have changed anything. I simply wasn't
ready to settle down. I could've handled things differently, though, and I am sorry for the way things ended
between us. Just know it wasn't because of anything
you'd done. That's entirely on me. Don't forget that.
Now, I think it's time for me to go check in with the
boys and grab a couple of hours' sleep while I still can.'
He got to his feet suddenly keen to reclaim that distance
between them before he was pushed to dig for a deeper
explanation. That panic was already rising in his chest
with the mere mention of his dad and he didn't want to
trigger the nightmares or the panic attacks by reliving
the horror again. It needed to end here. All of it. Including whatever misguided notion his sleep-deprived
mind had conjured up about trying to win Freya back.

* * *

The cold wind swirled in as Lucas opened the door, its icy fingers reaching in to grab Freya. Not even the blazing logs in the hearth could keep the chill from her bones and she huddled deeper into her blanket. Lucas's father had died and he hadn't told her. That said everything about the state their marriage had been in when he hadn't trusted her enough to confide in her and she'd never suspected he might've been grieving.

She knew what it was to mourn such a huge loss and how that sorrow was able to sneak up and steal your very breath in a moment of weakness. The searing raw pain was enough to make anyone want to walk away from it all and start over. That was exactly what she'd done by throwing herself into her nursing career when she'd lost her baby, never speaking of her little angel again. She hadn't even told Lucas because she'd never wanted him to think a baby of theirs would ever simply be to replace the one she'd lost. These secrets kept from one another had surely contributed to the breakdown of their relationship.

The timing left her questioning if his erratic behaviour could've been attributed to grief as well as the apparent lack of communication in their marriage.

Unfortunately, Lucas had reverted to type and shut her out again.

She jumped up from the couch with her comforter wrapped around her and ran after him. He was already knee-deep in the snow between the two cabins by the time she opened the door. As she ran out onto the wooden porch with only her thermal socks on her feet, it wasn't long before they started to turn numb but she wasn't going to let him go a second time without being given the chance to say her piece.

'I would've been there if you'd let me, Lucas,' she shouted, her voice carrying easily across the still, pre-dawn air. Even though their relationship was over, it was important he know that.

It stopped him in his tracks and the words hung between them, crystallising along with the tears on her cheeks as she waited for his response—an acknowledgement that he knew he wasn't alone in the world.

She watched as his head slumped forward, could see the wisps of his breathy sigh take flight into the frozen skies. The snow crunched beneath his feet as he slowly turned to face her.

'I know,' he said with a trembling smile and the glint of tears in his eyes, but it didn't stop him from walking away again.

He might have finally opened up a fraction about what had been going on behind the scenes at that difficult period but it hadn't eased that empty ache in her chest for the husband she'd lost or the family she'd never have. This early morning confessional hadn't changed anything—her marriage was still over. She still wasn't enough to make him happy.

CHAPTER FOUR

'THERE'S PAPER AND colouring pencils for you to draw Santa a picture of what you would like for Christmas, or I could write the list for you if you want?' Lucas made sure Scarlett had everything she needed at hand to complete her task as she took her seat at the wooden counter with the others.

The post office in Santa's Village was a hub of activity as kids and adults alike sent postcards home to their families as souvenirs and penned notes to the man they'd all come to visit. Lucas had never written a letter to Santa in his life and he wasn't about to start as an adult, but he was happy to write a few words on the back of a picture postcard for Scarlett's family as a memento. The address would be in her emergency contact details.

He jotted down the details of what they'd done so far and that they were excited about seeing Santa—a lie on his part but he would be happy once it was all over and he could go home—and got Scarlett to scrawl her name on the bottom before he handed it to a post-office elf. A glance across the table confirmed Freya was still engrossed in helping Hope, reaching for the glitter glue and showing no signs of leaving anytime soon. The tiny specks of silver dust glistening on her cheeks and hands gave him hope she'd recaptured a tiny bit of her inner child on this trip.

He'd hardly been able to look at her today for the same reason he'd been unable to respond appropriately to her after baring his soul. He had been afraid he'd break again as emotions had begun to overwhelm him. Freya had been the one person in his life who'd loved him unconditionally and he'd let go of her anyway. Regret was steadily eroding what was left of his much-needed defences but it wouldn't be good for either of them to let those old feelings for one another resurface when he knew he'd never deserved her love and would only ever bring her more misery.

The pile of picturesque postcards caught his eye, in particular the image of the forest at night with the Northern Lights casting an eerie green glow over the snowscape. It made him immediately think of Freya. She'd always talked with such reverence about seeing the lights one day, as if they held some sort of magical powers. It would be a shame if they went home without her wish coming true, and even if they did witness the phenomenon, the cold temperatures were known to freeze camera screens, so she mightn't even get to capture the event. He wanted her to have a small memento and at the same time give her some sort of explanation in writing because he hadn't made a very good job of delivering it in person so far.

Faced with the blank side of the card it was difficult

to come up with the words to both fill it and adequately express what he needed to say. Plus, he didn't exactly want his personal life to be coffee-break gossip in the post room. He took the coward's way out and started with the address—the home he was supposed to be sharing with his wife.

I'm sorry.

He could've left it at that but he'd said it a lot over the past twenty-four hours and it hadn't made a difference either to his conscience or Freya's pained expression every time she looked at him.

I always loved you, never wanted to hurt you, but I could never be the family man you need me to be. You deserve better.
Lucas xx

There seemed no need to mention the mental illness that had cost them their marriage when it was obvious they were going to go their separate ways again on their return. Even without his grief and depression keeping them apart, that basic conflict would remain— he couldn't imagine being part of the happy little family she wanted. He was a successful doctor because he'd studied hard and followed the lead of his mentors but he'd never had a role model to show him how to be a parent. It wasn't the kind of responsibility he would accept and hope for the best when he was a casualty himself of that selfish attitude towards parenting.

It was his fault their marriage was over but using the gory details of his trauma as an explanation now would inflict the very pain on Freya he'd been trying to avoid and only make her want to *understand* more. That was the kind of woman she was. One hint of what he'd been through and she'd already cried for him and tried to fix everything. For both of their sakes he needed to sever the ties, not strengthen them.

He handed the postcard over the counter, picture side up, hoping the elves either couldn't read English or were too discreet to judge the contents.

As he waited for the others to finish up so they could travel the final leg of the journey, there was one area of his life that suddenly became clearer. He'd put off making a decision about his temporary lodgings at Pete's because that had been easier than committing to change, but he could see now they all needed to move on. Remaining static would only prolong his grief for the life he could never have.

Even with the prospect of seeing Santa Claus in person it took some wrangling to get everyone to leave the warmth of the post-office room to go outside again. As soon as he had everyone lined up, one distracted child would invariably wander off.

'Sam, we've finished colouring in now. Can you come back and join the others. Please?' He wasn't averse to begging if it meant they could start the wagons rolling again.

Sam huffed back into line with his arms folded across his chest and a scowl creasing his forehead, just as a streak of pink took off running around the table. Lucas didn't know if it was over-excitement or being homesick that had set them off today. Whatever it was, it left him in no doubt he'd made the right decision in not having kids of his own. He didn't know how to handle them outside a hospital cubicle.

'I think we should start singing now so he can hear us coming the whole way through the forest.' Freya sidestepped any potential confrontation and took their errant charge's hand without any further fuss.

She was going to make a great mum. Which was exactly why she'd be better off without him weighing her down.

The rousing chorus of 'Jingle Bells' she started finally set them off out the door on a march towards the waiting sleighs. Lucas breathed a sigh of relief once their train of reindeer-drawn carriages was snaking through the lantern-lit woods, temper tantrums averted. It was all thanks to Freya. She was the peacemaker and the calm in any storm. Perhaps if he'd turned to her for guidance and support when the nightmares had begun tormenting him she might've helped quieten the chaos in his head before it had consumed him. Unfortunately his pride was a heavy price he hadn't wanted to pay.

As he watched her inside the dim interior of the log cabin, whispering the relevant info about each child to Santa as they stepped up for their gift, Lucas realised the outcome for their relationship was always going to have resulted in the same tragic ending. She was a ray of light in the shadows, her own excitement almost bubbling to the fore as she tried to keep the children quiet awaiting their turns. Too much of a free spirit, full of love and empathy, to be condemned to a childless lifetime shackled to his issues.

He stood at the back of the room detached from the scene before him, unlike Freya, who was right in the middle of it. The sounds of paper ripping and happy shrieks as the kids unwrapped their presents no longer angered him because he'd missed out on this unparalleled joy as a child but neither could he relate to it the way Freya seemed to. He was just kind of numb to it. The medication had kept him that way for a time, to quieten his thoughts and help him sleep, but he'd hated that zombielike existence and had been glad when therapy had helped him process what had happened to him so he could gradually be weaned off the antidepressants. He guessed this was his adjustment phase. Not unlike lying in a dark room for any length of time and suddenly having someone switch on a bright light. It had taken time to get used to his surroundings again and adapt accordingly. Life was different now but it simply wasn't the one he preferred because Freya was no longer in it.

'You were so good with them back there.' He made sure to acknowledge Freya's hand in the smooth proceedings as they filed back to the waiting sleighs without incident and watched the compliment pinch her cheeks.

'Similar mindset, I suspect. I was every bit as thrilled as they were to meet Father Christmas. Perhaps I'm not as immune to it all as I thought I was.'

That disarming smile he might not have seen again but for this trip made him ache for days gone by and lost for ever. There were some moments from his past he didn't want to erase from memory. All of them including Freya and that smile.

It made him forget everything but what it was to make her happy and the warmth spreading inside him in return. There was no separation, no audience, no cold, when she was glowing at him like this. It was only natural to want to reach out and touch his wife one last time.

'I'm glad you enjoyed yourself,' he said as he framed her face in his hands to capture that look of pure joy he'd thought he'd never see again.

Her lips parted on a gasp and he knew he wasn't the only one struck by that bolt of lightning every time they came into contact. A year ago he wouldn't have hesitated to lean in for the kiss he so desperately wanted but he no longer had claim to that privilege.

She covered his hands with her own and closed her eyes as if she was trying to preserve the moment too.

'Freya, I—' He watched her brow knit into a frown as he spoke and he realised nothing he could say would ever make things right again. He was the cause of that distress written so clearly on her face. Every single time.

'I think we should get back to the village before it gets any later.' He let his hands fall away with the last drop of hope he could ever make her happy again.

For one brief moment Freya had experienced that same contentment Hope seemed to find in her reindeer toy as she hugged it close all the way back to the village. In those few seconds Lucas had held her face cradled in his hands as though he would kiss her at any second, the world around her had shone brightly again. Then he'd let go of her and the shadows had crept once more over her heart to leave her shivering in the dimming light.

She'd been swept up into that optimistic euphoria along with the children. Just as they'd set aside their pain and uncertainty to lose themselves in the excitement, Freya had forgotten Lucas was no longer hers. She would never have relished a stranger's touch the way she had drunk in his. That was what he was now after all this time—a stranger, not her husband—and she'd do well to remember that for her own sake.

She didn't know what had prompted him to reach out when he'd appeared so detached at the cottage, standing at the back and observing rather than getting involved like all the others. Once more she found herself wondering what he'd been like as a child or, indeed, what went on in his head as an adult. That had been half of their problem. She'd never known what he'd been thinking because he would never share his thoughts with her.

As they returned to the village for some last-minute souvenir purchases, she put the last encounter down as an involuntary reaction to the climate. There was every possibility brain freeze had made them re-create some past memory with none of the original sentiment behind it. Or it could have been sympathy, pure and simple. He knew she was an old romantic and a complete sad case wishing this was all real and for the briefest time he'd let her believe they were still together, that she was happy again.

'Can we go on the big slide?' Hope was already running towards the giant ice slide that had been carved out in the centre of the tourist heaven. Judging by the queues lining up and down the hill it was the must-do event before returning home.

'Just once and then we'll have to find the others.' They'd all drifted off to do their own things for the last few minutes. Since the shops and restaurants were all in a circle, there was little chance of anyone getting lost and the bus to take them back to the airport was waiting just around the corner.

'Yay. Rudolph is coming too.' Hope waved her new friend in front of her face and made Freya wish she was that young again when a stuffed toy was enough to make you the happiest person in the world.

They waited as patiently as could be expected for a small child and a reluctant adult in subzero temperatures. Freya found herself watching the skies for those elusive green lights she'd been hoping to see to have made this trip personally worthwhile. So far it looked as though she was going home disappointed.

'I'm sorry you didn't get to see your lights on this trip.' Lucas's voice at her ear had her pulling her scarf tighter to defend against the chills currently rippling along the back of her neck. He picked up her train of thought so easily it was unnerving. Annoying. Inconvenient. Never more so than when she was trying to make sense of her feelings for him.

'It's okay. I think it's been eventful enough.' Managing a group of small children with special medical needs hyped up to meet Father Christmas had been enough of a challenge without throwing in her estranged husband and a lot of unresolved issues. The only thing she wanted to see more than the Northern Lights was her own bed where she could pull the duvet over her head and hide from these emotions which seemed to have reappeared with him.

She thought she saw a blush stain his cheeks but it was probably the cold biting rather than self-awareness of the upset he was causing her by being here. If he'd ever taken her feelings into consideration she wouldn't have spent the worst part of a year wondering what the hell had happened to them.

They moved uphill at an agonisingly slow pace and if it wasn't for the girls she knew they'd both be sitting at opposite ends of that airport bus, desperate to get away from each other as soon as possible. The one good thing to come out of this for her on a personal level was that the mystery of his whereabouts was finally solved, even if the details remained sketchy. It was closure of a kind.

She held Hope's hand, as Lucas did Scarlett's, as they took their positions at the top of the slide and pushed off. There were squeals of delight from the smaller passengers as they slid to the bottom of the hill all too quickly.

'Again!' they chorused.

'Sorry, girls. It's time to go home.' Lucas got to his feet and shot out a hand to help Freya. It would be churlish to refuse it yet she didn't want him touching her and upsetting her equilibrium all over again. She reconciled herself with the fact they were both wearing gloves again and there would be no further skin-on-skin contact.

'Aww.' Scarlett and Hope's sulking began in earnest now they knew this was the end of their snowy fun.

'Just think of all the things you have to tell everyone.' Freya did her best to get them to focus on the positives. At least until they were on the bus and on their way to the airport. She could do without any bad-tempered meltdowns on top of everything else.

'I liked the reindeer.' Hope shrugged, easily distracted with her precious gift still clutched to her chest.

'Well, I like the slide.' Scarlett stuck out her tongue in an uncharacteristic bout of petulance.

Freya supposed they'd had it easy up until now. A busy weekend with small children, and her ex-husband, was always going to have its testing moments and this was shaping up to be one of them.

'We've all enjoyed different things, Scarlett, but it's time to go.' Lucas tried his best to coax her away from the bottom of the slide before the next lot of eager thrill seekers made their way down.

'Yes. We've had a good time. Let's not spoil it now.' As nightmarish as some aspects of this weekend had been for her, he was right—there'd been flashes of true enjoyment for her too. It was a shame the spectre of her dead marriage was always going to haunt any good memories.

Freya tried to take her hand but Scarlett wrapped

her arms around her body and shook her head. 'I want to go again!'

Even if they'd had time to join the queue again Freya knew she couldn't give in to this type of behaviour. She didn't want to start a trend amongst the rest of the children when they were about to embark on their long journey home.

Before she had time to put her foot down any further, Scarlett turned on her heel and ran back towards the snaking line waiting to slide.

'Scarlett, wait!' Freya made a grab for her but she dodged out of reach and ran back across the bottom of the slide just as the next group of people came barrelling down.

Scarlett was too busy scowling back to notice the long-legged teen behind her. In painfully slow motion her little legs were swept out from beneath her so she fell back, her head hitting the smooth ice with a blood-curdling crack.

Lucas's cry matched Freya's as they helplessly watched the scene unfold, getting there too late to prevent the fall.

'Scarlett? Scarlett? Talk to me, sweetheart. Are you okay?' Lucas was on his knees at once, checking her airways were clear and trying to get a response. He placed his hands on either side of her head to stabilise her neck. In circumstances such as these they had to treat the patient as if there'd been a spinal injury.

Freya saw a small trail of blood on the ice and when she parted Scarlett's hair she found a small gash on her scalp.

'I'll treat the head wound.' She grabbed the back-pack containing the first-aid kit. That kind of knock to the head could do untold damage and wasn't some-thing either of them would treat lightly. Scarlett's eyes were open but unfocused and her body stiff.

'Scarlett, can you hear me?' Freya covered the wound with a sterile gauze dressing and tried to keep her connected but her blue eyes suddenly rolled back in her head and her limbs began to twitch uncontrol-lably as a seizure took hold of her body.

'Scarlett, we're going to get some help for you, sweetheart.' Lucas summoned over one of the other nurses, who was passing by, and asked her to take Hope away from the scene and phone for an ambu-lance.

Freya knew from experience it was better to get one here sooner than later in case they needed oxygen or meds such as benzodiazepines to end the seizure if it went on for longer than five minutes. The head injury was going to need to be treated too.

'Everything's going to be all right, Scarlett. We're right here.' Freya held the gauze to her wound, pray-ing this ended as quickly as it had begun. A prolonged seizure could starve the brain of oxygen, and the lon-ger it lasted, the less likely it was to stop on its own. They'd known this was a possibility, of course, but the whole point of the trip had been to show the children their conditions didn't have to limit their experiences. It was unfortunate they hadn't made it back to the UK before reality had hit.

Lucas checked his watch. 'That's longer than five

minutes. I'm going to need to review the protocol sheet and the buccal midazolam.'

As carers for Scarlett during this trip they'd both familiarised themselves with the written protocol provided by the consultant treating her condition should such an emergency arise but the laminate had to be rechecked every time emergency medicine had to be administered. She tossed the bag containing the medication to Lucas then took over the job of trying to keep their patient's head and neck stabilised.

He confirmed all the details were correct on the package before he opened the pre-filled syringe. The sedative, which came in the form of a sugar-free syrup, was supposed to have a calming effect on the brain and was often able to end a seizure.

He opened Scarlett's mouth and made sure the buccal cavity between the cheek and gums was clear before he administered the required dose, then checked his watch again. It was vital they keep an eye on the time to ensure they gave it sufficient time to take effect before they administered a second dose.

'Hopefully the ambulance will get here soon.' There was always a possibility of breathing difficulties with these emergency drugs and only so much they could do out here. If they couldn't stop the fitting she'd need to be put on a ventilator to help her breathe until she recovered.

'We'll be with her until it does.' Lucas stripped off his ski suit and used it to keep Scarlett warm.

Freya saw him shiver as he covered the child with his outerwear. When it came to helping others he always stepped up to the plate without a second thought for himself. That was why it was so hard to reconcile his heartless actions of the past with the man now kneeling in the snow, comforting a sick child.

Freya allowed herself a fleeting pang of self-pity for the husband and father she could've had, should've had by her side for more than one weekend, but she had to snap out of it quickly because she was no longer the one suffering here. Scarlett needed her and Lucas to work together to make this as painless as possible for all of them.

'I'm so sorry you had to come all the way out here.' Freya couldn't apologise enough to the distraught parents who'd arrived at the hospital in the dead of night. This wasn't how any of them had wanted the trip to end.

'We know she's in good hands but we wanted to see her for ourselves.' Scarlett's mother rushed down the corridor with her, understandably anxious to see her daughter.

'Of course.' Freya would've reacted exactly the same way if it had been her child lying hurt in a strange hospital.

The others had flown home hours ago after a brief stop at the hospital for an update and to drop off the luggage, which would now have to be checked onto a later flight. Lucas was the medical lead, so he'd immediately volunteered to stay behind, but Scarlett had been under Freya's care from the start and there was no way she was leaving the country without her. She was feeling bad enough that she'd had to hand over Hope's care to Gillian for the journey home, even though she couldn't possibly be in two places at once.

'How is she? You said on the phone she'd hit her head before the seizure...'

'The doctor is just checking in on her now.' The fitting had ceased before the ambulance had arrived but Scarlett's head injury was still worrying. They'd ordered CT scans on arrival, the results of which might require further investigation or referral to a neurosurgeon if there were signs of any damage. It was a necessary precaution.

On cue, Lucas strode towards them and shook hands with the late-night arrivals. 'Lucas Brodie. You'll be pleased to know all Scarlett's scans came back clear but she needed a couple of stitches to her head wound. They're just keeping her in overnight for observation.'

'Thank goodness she's all right.' Freya's heart lifted as soon as she heard there'd been no long-lasting damage. Without any extra complications, and providing there were no more seizures during the night, Scarlett would most likely be discharged the next day.

'Can we see her?' This time it was the father who was eager for first-hand verification of his daughter's health.

'She's resting now, but the staff said it was fine to sit with her for a few minutes. The doctor in charge of her care is with her now if you'd like to speak to him yourself.' That frown, which had been on Lucas's face since Scarlett's fall, finally evened out as he delivered the good news.

'Thank you, Doctor.' The couple bustled away as soon as Lucas pointed them in the right direction.

'Scarlett's really going to be okay?' Freya wanted clarification he hadn't been sugar-coating anything for her parents' benefit.

'There's still a few tests to run in the morning but all the signs are good.' His hand was cool on hers as he reached out to reassure her and she remembered his earlier sacrifice for his patient.

'You're freezing!' They'd been indoors long enough now that he should've warmed up. It showed how cold he must've been out there in the snow if he was still in the process of defrosting.

'I'm fine.' He tried to snatch his hand away from her grasp, probably embarrassed that she'd discovered he was human after all.

Her inner nurse took over from common sense insisting his discomfort should be of no interest to her.

'You are not. You're practically purple with cold. It's not going to help anyone if you end up with hypothermia, is it?' she scolded, rubbing his palms between both of hers, trying to generate some heat.

Far from blanching at the telling-off, he seemed amused by her fussing over him and her blood boiled that her concern should be a source of entertainment. This whole situation would've been a lot easier if she didn't care whether he froze to death or not. She rubbed his upper arms, hoping to get his circulation going and perhaps give him a friction burn from his sweater. At least her sudden sadistic streak would take her mind off the rounded biceps bunched beneath her sweeping hands and the vivid memories of the body she'd known so well once upon a time.

This was supposed to be about his survival, not her copping a feel.

'If you're *really* worried, I hear that skin-to-skin contact works best at transferring body heat.' The skin crinkled at the corners of his eyes as he teased her and she gave him a playful slap to hide the surge of hormones heating her own body at the suggestion.

'I think you'll live.' She took a step back so she could focus again and watched Lucas run his hand—which was now a healthier pink colour—through his hair, looking every bit as ruffled as he'd made her.

'We're going to stay with Scarlett here tonight. You two should go back to the hotel and get some rest.' Scarlett's father popped his head around the corner and offered them some unexpected respite. As much as every fibre in Freya's body was begging her for rest, she had a responsibility to the little girl that she wasn't ready to abandon.

'We couldn't possibly—'

'I insist. There's no need for all of us to be here. We appreciate everything you've done but go and get some sleep.' He didn't hang around to listen to further argument and Freya was too tired to fight common sense. There was nothing more they could do for Scarlett tonight and Lucas was quick to point out they'd be more help if they got some rest before they accompanied the family on the journey home again. He headed to Reception to use the landline and call the hotel but the heavy sigh on his return didn't fill her full of confidence about their last-minute booking.

'We're here for the night.'

'What do you mean? Surely someone can give us a lift back to the cabins?' This definitely hadn't been on the itinerary but it wouldn't be a hardship to spend another night in Lapland luxury.

'I've just called them. They're booked out. Apparently they had another party arrive straight after we checked out this afternoon.' He shrugged an apology but it wasn't his fault or anyone else's that they'd been stranded here. It was simply bad luck.

'I don't have a problem slumming it in a regular hotel. I could sleep standing up right now. As lovely as the cabin was, I'll settle for four walls and a bed.' She yawned and stretched, her body giving in to tiredness now that they knew Scarlett was safe and sound and her parents were with her.

'Any hotels within trudging distance are booked up too. I guess this isn't the time, or place, for unscheduled overnight stays.' It was obvious he'd done his best to find them accommodation but it wasn't as if they could just check into the nearest bed and breakfast out here in the wintry wilds.

'Thanks for trying. I guess we really are stuck here for the night.' She eyed the mismatched plastic chairs, which were the only apparent visitor accommodation. The local facility didn't have access to a family room, which a bigger hospital in the main town might've had for parents and guardians keeping a vigil.

'As you know, I'm very low-maintenance...' She'd

never made outrageous demands of her husband. Only that he honour the vows they'd taken on their wedding day to stay with her, and that had turned out to be too much to ask of him.

There might have been some who'd have screamed and hollered at the prospect of a night sleeping on a chair and stamped their feet until a bed was made available, but she didn't expect anything of anyone any more. She'd do what she'd done for the past year and get on with it. The holdall containing her clothes wouldn't make much of a pillow but she tried to pummel it into submission enough to rest her head on.

'I know you deserve more,' Lucas muttered low enough under his breath she wasn't sure she was supposed to hear.

It didn't matter if he was referring to the sleeping arrangements or her choice of husband when she was stuck with both.

'Are you going to stand there all night?' She had her head turned away from him but she could sense him hovering nearby and that meant there was even less chance of her getting to sleep.

'No, and you're not going to spend the night in that chair either.' The hard edge to his voice and the sound of him stalking back towards Reception had Freya scrambling back to an upright position to see what was going to happen next.

He walked with such purpose and authority it set her pulse skipping after him. It reminded her of the self-assurance that had drawn her to him from the start and with it the sickening realisation she would still follow him to the ends of the earth if he asked her to. Regardless of the fact he'd ripped her heart out once already, she remained a lost cause when it came to Lucas Brodie.

She didn't know what more fate had in store for her during this trip but she prayed she was going to make it through the next twenty-four hours with the rest of her heart still intact.

CHAPTER FIVE

'THIS IS TOO MUCH, Lucas!' Freya's objection didn't quite gel with her actions as she spun around, arms out-stretched, staring up at the sky in wonder like a child seeing snow for the first time.

He knew it was everything she could want here and worth every penny he'd slapped onto his credit card. A glass igloo wasn't merely a step up from crashing on plastic chairs in a corridor; it was a no-expense-spared apology, his attempt to make up for some of the hurt he'd caused her in the past.

With extensive Internet surfing and numerous phone calls courtesy of the receptionist it had turned out there was one last accommodation option available and he'd jumped at this opportunity for Freya's sake. The small igloo village surrounded by pine trees and little else was the ideal place for an Aurora Borealis watch.

'I thought it would be good for you to take back some nice memories of this trip.' And of him. He didn't want her last thoughts of him to be tied to feelings of discomfort and disappointment.

'I'm not going to forget this in a hurry.' She stopped

spinning under the glass dome ceiling to give him a bright, unguarded smile and out-twinkled the stars in the dark skies above them. The sight of her just about stopped his heart beating. He'd be content to die right here and now with the thought he'd been able to make her happy again with this one act.

'It's kind of like glamping in the Arctic.' He dumped their bags in the corner of the bedroom/living area. The one downside of his magnanimous gesture was the lack of space. It didn't correlate with the notion of maintaining some distance after their heart-to-heart last night.

As pretty and warm as their little glass bubble was, there was no chance of skulking off to his own room and avoiding her until sunrise. Apart from the separate toilet and shower it was essentially one round bedroom. No TV, no Internet, no distraction from his beautiful companion.

He collapsed down onto one of the beds. At least they weren't expected to share because that really would have been a step too far for both of them. The only thing that stopped it being too claustrophobic was the transparent ceiling and the view above his head of the endless sky. He hoped more than ever that Freya would get her light show and save them from having to make more conversation than he was comfortable with.

'Do you think people can see in?' Freya whispered, as though there was someone eavesdropping on her every word.

'Can you see anyone else?' The only thing in his peripheral vision were snow-covered tree limbs and the orange glow of their distant neighbours. The architects had clearly taken the privacy of their guests into consideration for this experience.

'Well…no,' she conceded, and began to unzip her ski suit now she was satisfied she wouldn't be giving a peep show.

Although he doubted there were any more interesting sights than her stripping off her Abominable Snowman outfit. More like adorable snowman. Lucas tried to distract his wayward thoughts from the sound of her zip. Not even the spectacle of the Northern Lights would compete with the body he knew intimately beneath that suit.

They both knew that watching her take off her clothes had been one of his favourite pastimes.

'How do they keep the snow and ice off the windows?' she carried on, oblivious to his increasing discomfort.

'Heated glass. Same principle as the underfloor heating, I guess. We've got all the mod cons.' There was a panel by the bed and he couldn't resist pushing the switch to see what other surprises awaited. Although if it turned out it was one of those vibrating beds he might end up having to pitch his own tent outside in the snow. Bar the single beds, this already had all the hallmarks of a honeymoon suite rather than an almost divorced couple forced into spending an awkward night together.

He waited for the seventies' motel jiggling to begin and was almost disappointed by the slow and partial rise of the mattress.

'Is that for a better view?' Freya arched an eyebrow at him as he rose to an almost sitting position in time to see her unpack her night things.

'Probably,' he mumbled, and promptly lowered himself back down again. The idea had been to provide her with a vista to wipe last night's discussion from her mind but he'd inadvertently engineered another sleepless night for himself, having Freya so close. Not only was the thought of her right here next to him a distraction but there was also the worry the nightmares would return.

He hadn't had one for quite some time but there was no absolute cure for the anxiety he still encountered from time to time and there was the possibility all this talk of the past would prey on his subconscious if he drifted off. Since leaving Freya's bed he'd slept alone, but Peter, his flatmate and saviour, had kept him informed of his night terrors at the time. Sometimes his stress manifested while he was sleeping and the sweating, the screaming and crying he'd suffered at the onset of his illness were not attributes he particularly wanted to share with her. They mightn't be together any more but that didn't mean his ego would accept sharing his weakness with her.

As Freya disappeared into the bathroom to change, Lucas plumped his pillows and prepared himself for a long night, thankful his experience of working night shifts had built up his stamina for such occasions.

He couldn't resist a sneak peek as she stole back to bed, or the snort laugh when he saw what she was wearing.

'What? I packed for warmth and comfort, not company.' She dived beneath the covers but it was too late; he'd already witnessed the fleecy reindeer onesie.

'Good.' It came out gruffer than he'd intended, or he'd any right to, at the thought of her having a bed partner. The mere suggestion of another man sharing her bed, or her usual choice of skimpy nightwear, had him frowning. He didn't know how he'd cope if and when their divorce finally went through. They hadn't actually discussed the future, yet he couldn't expect Freya to put her life on hold any longer. It was a real gut punch to finally face up to the fact she could be with someone else. He might just have to flee the country to remain in denial.

'Aren't you going to get ready for bed?'

'I don't wear pyjamas, as you very well know, Freya.' He'd said it with the intention of making her blush, making her imagine him naked in her bed and put all thoughts of any other man out of her head. Of course, she mightn't have the same interest in his love life as he apparently had in hers but she hadn't given him that impression thus far.

Not that he could have his cake and eat it. There was no way he could keep his dark, desperate past to himself and his wife happy at the same time. He'd tried that and failed miserably.

He reached out and flicked the light switch off, plunging them into darkness but for the glittering stars above their heads. He would just lie here uncomfortable and brooding until the sun came up. If he couldn't see her he wouldn't think about her. That was the way it was supposed to work. At least, that was what he'd told himself for the past year.

'There hasn't been anyone else since you, Lucas.' Her admission in the dark reached in past all the bravado to see deep inside his soul. No one else had that ability to expose his vulnerable internal workings and that was what terrified him. She could've listed a whole string of lovers and cut him to the quick but, unlike him, it wasn't in her nature to inflict unnecessary pain or cruelty towards another being.

Lucas got out of bed and walked towards the bathroom, unable to hear any more as the weight of guilt threatened to crush him. Bedcovers rustled behind him as Freya turned onto her side, away from the perfect night and her far-from-perfect husband. He could almost taste the saltiness of her tears on his tongue.

The bathroom mirror mocked him with the younger face of his father. He stripped off his shirt and splashed himself with cold water to take away the sting of his burning shame. Now he was faced with the prospect of having to let her go again, he was questioning if he'd even made the right decision first time around. His anxiety had been so overwhelming then, imagining the worst in every situation, it was possible he'd acted rashly and prematurely thrown their marriage away. If it had been the right course of action surely neither of them should still be in so much agony now?

There was only one way he could attempt to make amends to Freya for the wrong he'd done her, even if he was sweating at the very thought.

The sheets were cool on his naked back as he lay down on his bed and prepared his confession.

'I haven't been with anyone else since you either, Freya.' It was a big confession to make when he knew it would raise all sorts of other questions about their lost year but he owed it to her to return her honesty.

'Then why did you leave me?' Her voice was but a breath in the night, yet he had to close his eyes to steel himself from the blow.

'I was going through some mental health problems. I didn't think you should have to go through them with me and thought I was doing the right thing by leaving. I was so messed up I guess I wasn't thinking about anything clearly.' Silence swallowed him whole.

It really was quiet out here, his painful admission the only sound in the forest. In different circumstances he would've found the setting a tranquil retreat from the daily grind. Not tonight. Not in his head and definitely not in his heart.

'Why couldn't you have told me? I'm a nurse, for goodness' sake. I would've helped you get whatever treatment you needed.' Her frustration at him was justified when he'd recently begun questioning his own decision-making at that time.

'I didn't really know what was going on in my head. The news of my dad's death opened up a Pandora's box of memories and emotions I apparently hadn't dealt with. I didn't want him to be a part of my life with you so I never told you he was a mean drunk who should never have been allowed to look after a dog, never mind raise a child. I think the only reason the authorities never got involved was because I was so good at hiding the bruises. For some reason I thought it was better to have him as a parent than have none at all.' He'd been so desperate to cling on to what had been left of his family he'd accepted daily beatings as normal life. Not to mention the appalling conditions and the empty cupboards of the filthy house he'd been expected to call home.

'Lucas, I'm so, so sorry.'

He didn't take any pleasure in her gasp of horror or any relief in finally sharing the agony of his childhood. It simply brought back that horrible roller-coaster rise and fall of nausea at recalling it, even if he was at least able to discuss it now without breaking down.

He coughed away the ragged ball of emotion threatening to block his airways. 'I left home when I could, moved into a hostel and held down two jobs to put myself through medical school. I mistakenly thought I could escape my father with hard work and determination to make a success of my life, but news of his death brought back a lot of those painful memories and kind of hit me for six.'

'You should have told me. Maybe we could've got through it together.'

'I think I had some sort of breakdown… I couldn't think, or sleep, without images of him rearing in my head. The sound of his drunken ramblings, blaming me for my mum leaving; the smell of his foul breath as he loomed over me and even the shame I felt going to school in dirty, hand-me-down clothes—it all came rushing back at once and refused to leave my thoughts.

I was just so full of rage and shame…and wanting to be free of it all.' He let that sink in so he didn't have to spell out that for a moment he'd believed there was only one way of escaping the pain.

'Even me?'

There was a creak as she shifted in her bed. To look at him? To get up and lock herself in the bathroom away from his self-pity? It didn't matter. Now he'd opened the box, there was no way of stuffing all the secrets back inside.

He let out a long sigh. 'I never wanted to be without you but I didn't want to drag you into that darkness. I took it with me. In my head, at least. I know my actions seem selfish but I couldn't see any other way out. His death triggered flashbacks, turned me back into that frightened little boy, afraid of his own shadow. What kind of husband would that have made me?'

'Mine.'

He hadn't heard her cross the room, didn't know she was there until the mattress dipped beside him. He didn't know he'd been crying until she wiped the tears away for him.

That small act of compassion, that comforting physical contact he'd been missing for so long, finally burst the dam, and the emotions he'd thought he'd dealt with came tumbling out once more. This time it wasn't the liquid pain of his childhood pouring down his face; it was grief for his marriage and losing the woman he'd loved.

She slid her arms around him, lifting his torso off the bed and forcing him into a hug. He wanted to resist, to keep hold of what little there was left of his dignity, but he'd forgotten how it felt to be loved. If he'd ever really known it at all until now.

She pressed her warm cheek tightly against his as though she was physically trying to transfer some of his pain to herself. Of course she understood, she was a nurse, but he'd never wanted to be treated as her patient.

'You got the help…the treatment you needed?' Freya swallowed several times before she got the words out, and Lucas could sense her already attempting to find that professional distance again.

He buried his nose in her hair and took a deep breath, wanting to savour her sweet scent before he let go of her in case he never had this chance to be this close to her ever again.

'The strong medication wiped me out for the first while. They dulled the pain, quietened the memories but they also numbed the world around me, left me unable to function in any emotional capacity. It was the counselling, talking it all out, learning to process what had happened, that finally brought me back to the man I used to be. I'm just sorry it took so long.' Perhaps if he'd fought harder to get back towards the light neither of them would've suffered so much for so long. They might've even saved their marriage or at least found a better way to end it.

'You're here now,' she said, her smile shaky in the moonlight, unable to settle fully on her lips. He could see the steady river of sorrow for him glinting on her face, though she tried to hide it.

'And this was exactly what I'd been trying to avoid.'
He brushed away her tears the way she had for him.
The weight of his secrets might have finally been lifted
from his shoulders but he'd never wanted to dump it
on hers. He leaned his forehead against hers, wishing
they'd stood a chance from the outset.

If he closed his eyes he could still imagine it.

When his lips found hers he wanted to believe he'd
really come home again.

Freya had thought her heart would never ache as much
as it had the day he'd left her but knowing now what
he'd gone through she was worried it might just break
for him. For the little boy, so alone and scared, and for
her husband, in so much pain she wanted to take it all
away. His hand, still cupping her face, tilted her mouth
towards him and kissing him seemed the most natural
thing in the world, both giving and taking comfort in
the soft exchange.

She rested her palms on his chest, not realising he'd
stripped off his top half in the dark. That first touch of
his naked skin under her fingertips was electric and
her erogenous zones immediately lit up as she reac-
quainted herself with the smooth undulations of her
husband's muscular torso.

She'd intended to offer him support, remind him he
didn't have to be alone, yet now all she wanted to do
was give in to desire and block out everything except
their need for each other.

He teased her lips apart with the tip of his tongue,
gently exploring the boundaries. Freya's stronger, more

cynical subconscious, which had kept her standing this past year, popped into her mind's eye, wagged a finger and shook its head. Everything in her body language was screaming for her to back away. It was no competition for her soft-hearted inner romantic, who just wanted to love her husband and have him love her in return.

They'd both been through hell and they deserved to take some solace where they could find it. In each other.

She ignored her arm-folding, tutting common sense to get to know her husband intimately again. The tentative kiss grew more confident, more insistent as she met his tongue instead of shying away from his advance. She didn't want to think about the past, not even what the future might hold past this night together. Her thoughts, her body were consumed with the need for this, for him, and the knowledge this chemistry hadn't fizzled out.

His lips were everywhere, setting the skin at her cheeks, her throat, her neck on fire. His breathing was as heavy as hers, full of want and need, and hot enough to melt the glass walls around them.

Committed to the moment, she let her hands travel down his lean torso, every inch of skin as tight as a drum. He'd always been trim but there was more definition, an edge to him she'd never encountered before. It told of hard work and dedication during his struggle to survive.

Lucas sucked in a breath and stilled against her as she reached the waistband of his trousers, casting a shadow of panic over her desire that she'd done the wrong thing by trying to rush this. Her sudden haste had been a combination of pent-up lust, which had been steadily rising since he'd stepped on board the plane, and a need to avoid overthinking this.

She froze, her fingers tangled in his waistband, her pulse racing, as though she'd been caught with her hand in the cookie jar.

'It's, uh, been a while,' he admitted, and she could almost feel him cringing with the confession there was no reason why it should embarrass him.

The thought of him with another woman had been the cause of many sleepless nights and to hear the truth eased part of that associated pain. The separation and subsequent months of abstinence would've made anyone a little nervous, including her, but passion had never been a problem for them.

'Good.' She smoothed her palm over the crotch of his trousers and gave his burgeoning erection a playful squeeze.

His sexy groan made it all the way down to her belly along with her zipper as he peeled her nightwear away as sexily as though she was wearing nothing but the finest silk. He kissed his way confidently across her exposed skin, and her temperature spiked, any theory that their chemistry could be anything other than explosive proving completely unfounded.

With Lucas's assistance her clothes fell to the floor, leaving her naked and exposed to his hungry mouth licking and sucking and leaving her gasping for more. She lay back on the bed, shaking with need and wondering how this had ended up about her, but distraction had always been one of his special skills. Among others.

He moulded her breast easily into the palm of his hand and she fitted there just as perfectly as she always had. Arousal coursed through her body as he plucked one tight bud between his finger and thumb, leaving her content to change the subject on this occasion.

For a short time. There was only so much a girl could take before she was practically pleading for more.

'Lucas...' Okay, a year without him meant she wasn't averse to asking for more.

She'd missed this intimacy, not only since he'd left but also in those last weeks of their marriage when he'd been so emotionally distant. Now that he'd given her some understanding of where his head had been back then, and they'd made that reconnection, she felt as though she'd got back the man she loved. Even if only for tonight.

At one time she'd wanted him to suffer but that had been before she'd discovered the full facts behind his departure and the extent of his true anguish. No one should've had to endure what he'd gone through either as a child or an adult. He deserved peace and a little fun. They both did.

'There isn't much room here,' Lucas said as he manoeuvred his body on top of hers in the tiny single bed built for stargazing, not reuniting past lovers.

The rough, stretched fabric of his crotch rubbed against her sensitive mound, teasing her folds until she was sure she'd climax purely with the memory of what he could do to her.

'Yeah, we need to get rid of these.' Her increased libido was making her brave but also impatient to make the most of what little time they might have together.

He levered himself up off the bed slightly, granting her access to his fly, which she negotiated in record time to liberate him. That perfect, familiar epicentre of his manhood sprang free as she nudged the remainder of his clothes over his backside and down his legs.

She giggled as he wriggled on top, trying to kick his clothes off, their naked bodies accidentally thrusting together at the most intimate of places before they rolled completely off the bed. If anything, this proved neither of them had been perfecting their seduction techniques in their interim. It was a tad more uncoordinated and ungainly now than they'd been that first time when he'd practically swept her off her feet and into his bed but she found it heartening. They were learning together like two inexperienced teens, anxious but eager to reach that first sacred destination together.

Everything about this moment—the fun and the passion—reminded her of that life they'd once had together and everything they'd lost. The tears pricking her eyes told her how much more she was missing Lucas from her life than the family they'd never had together.

CHAPTER SIX

LUCAS HAD NEVER thought he would feel as vulnerable as he had sitting in his counsellor's office, crying and spilling his guts about the punishments his alcoholic father had dished out to him for the purported crime of being born. Acknowledging to Freya it had been a while since he'd *performed* ran a close second.

Thankfully his body's primitive response at the sight of his naked wife had quickly allayed any worries that his masculinity might have somehow been compromised during the course of his recovery.

This night together wasn't something he had planned beyond the logistics of their accommodation but he'd never expected her to give him another chance any more than he'd intended to tell her about the demons that had driven him away. Despite the damage they'd suffered, there was obviously still a special connection between them that refused to be broken.

He mightn't be the smooth operator he'd once been, but being with Freya felt so right nothing else mattered but lying here with her. Those secrets he'd kept had meant holding back a part of himself in the course of their relationship but after baring his soul he now had the freedom to love her the way she'd deserved all along.

As Freya let her hands drift over the trunk of his body, and bit her lip as she dared ever lower, there was no questioning her desire for him either. This wasn't pity over the hard times he'd shared with her, or sleeping with him for old times' sake. She was seeing him as the man he'd never thought he would be again—her husband.

Lucas tangled her hair in his hands and kissed her as though they were the last two people on earth. Tonight, in this glass bubble, they were. Their mouths crashed together and the shadowy recesses of the past faded into insignificance against that need to make love to his wife.

He'd missed her, he loved her, and as their bodies joined together, he knew there would never be anyone else for him.

Those nights he'd spent without her, those vivid dreams when he'd imagined her lying next to him, only to find his bed achingly empty—he channelled it all through his body into hers. He withdrew and plunged back inside her again and again, each time feeling like the first.

The quickening clench and release of her inner muscles around him and the tilt of her hips meeting his started the pressure building inside him too. She was clutching at his back, her head thrown back in ecstasy whilst his every muscle quivered in anticipation of her climax.

Freya's visceral cry of release took him by surprise. Although they'd always been passionate together, he'd never heard her so vocal. It was a primal scream of unleashed pain and passion from a very different woman than the one he'd left behind, and it shook him to his very core. She was stronger, more self-assured than he remembered, which made her sexier than ever and brought his orgasm swiftly. That gunshot intensity reverberated through his body with such force he thought he'd never recover.

Relief and a sense of peace claimed him, body and soul, as he let go. As if the year of emotional turmoil had physically left him, and he'd finally been liberated from the past. He didn't have the energy for anything more than to lie here on the floor, holding Freya close and wishing this could last for ever.

'I've missed this,' she whispered into his chest.

'Me too.' Lucas eventually summoned up enough strength to snag the duvet off the bed and pull it over them for the night. He knew he'd sleep well tonight with her wrapped around him like ivy around a tree trunk. There would be no nightmares or waking up in a cold sweat in a too-empty bed. Tonight he had everything he wanted. For now he was content to believe it could last.

Freya wanted to stretch out every muscle and revel in that glorious post-sex ache winding through her limbs, but that would entail breaking contact with Lucas's warm, familiar body and she wasn't ready to do that yet.

Right now she should be lying like a starfish in her double bed alone, in the home where she'd always imagined their family. This seemed a much nicer place to curl up for the night. Sleeping with her ex hadn't been part of her plan but neither had this whole extended stay.

Would it have happened if he hadn't been honest with her? She couldn't say, but finally opening up to her, exposing that vulnerable side he'd tried to hide throughout their short-lived marriage, had given her the excuse to act on those feelings for him that had never gone away. The husband who'd walked out on her was also a man who'd been in turmoil himself and on the verge of goodness knew what. Seeing and hearing the evidence of that trauma for herself had immediately demanded her forgiveness. It wasn't a time she would ever forget, or easily move forward from, but at least she understood why it had happened.

She could see now how consumed she'd been with her own past to remain so oblivious to his pain. Her grief over losing her baby had driven her to the point of obsession of having another one when she should've been happy she'd found someone special. Both of them had let the unhappy previous lives they'd led contaminate the one they could've had together.

This quiet afterglow was tinged at the edges with a little sadness. If they'd explored this honesty during the course of their relationship they might have avoided the nuclear fallout of their break-up. A year ago this conversation would have swung her into action on his behalf, to save her husband's mental health

before things became too much for him. She would've
got him the professional help he'd needed, been there
when he'd needed to rage or cry, been someone to comfort him for once in his life. Peter had had to step up as
his nursemaid, his confidant and apparent bodyguard,
fending off hysterical abandoned wives he'd deemed
might damage him more. He'd been the one to save
him and not her, because Lucas hadn't let her. Whilst
she was grateful for those who had intervened on his
behalf, it had cost her her place in his life and a year
of being in divorce limbo.

Lucas laced his fingers through hers and brought
them to his lips. There was no need for words when his
love was there in the gentleness of his kiss, his apology for ever causing her pain there in his eyes. Nothing could change what had happened to either of them
but she was hoping now that they could start looking
forward instead of behind them.

The new chapter of their lives dawned with a strange
emerald light as their cosy bubble became bathed in
an ethereal glow from above.

'Oh, Lucas!' She sat up, clutching the quilt to her
chest as the jewelled skies shifted from midnight blue
to green, and back again, with the phenomenon she'd
always dreamed of seeing. The dancing arcs of changing light from the Aurora Borealis helped ensure this
would be one trip to truly remember.

He rose with her, the heat of his torso at her back.
'You'd think I planned this,' he said with a laugh.

'You didn't?' It all seemed too perfect to have happened by accident. Especially after the year of hell they'd lived through.

He wrapped his arms around her waist and nuzzled into her neck. 'I'll happily take credit for finding your Northern Lights for you but I swear everything tonight has come as much as a surprise to me as it has to you.'

Given his personal revelations tonight, she didn't doubt that. Lucas Brodie was a proud man; there was no greater display of that than when he'd left their marital home rather than admit he was going through a tough time. She didn't know what difference tonight would make to their relationship status, if anything, but for now she simply wanted to sit here and soak up what was left of the magic. The morning and a heavy dose of reality would rear its head soon enough.

A long, leisurely lie-in and breakfast in bed with his wife would've been heavenly but the sunrise brought with it a different list of priorities for Lucas. The first thing he did was to make his way back to the main hotel to phone the hospital and check on their patient. Once he'd been assured she hadn't suffered any more seizures and would be discharged as soon as possible, he started organising the return trip.

Last night had opened a whole new world of possibilities he'd thought no longer available to him and he couldn't wait to get home again. Rather than pack up and move on to pastures new, he'd seen a glimpse of the old life he'd had with Freya and he wanted it back. Now there were no more secrets to keep them apart and they obviously still had feelings for each other, there was a chance they might be able to make their marriage work.

It was the first time since news of his father had triggered his illness that he was actually looking forward to the future. One hopefully with Freya in it. Those early months had been about survival and more recently the recovery of his health and career. Now he wanted to make plans for the married life they should've had together. Including a Christmas free from bleak memories and dark moods. He had a lot of making up to do for last year and now he was beginning to understand the excitement the children had felt leading up to seeing Father Christmas. Suddenly he couldn't wait for all those glitzy trimmings to appear around the house or the smell of turkey and stuffing as he walked through the door if it meant he was spending Christmas with his wife instead of being alone in someone's spare room.

By the time he returned to the igloo with coffee and pastries, Freya was washed, dressed and all evidence of their tryst had been tidied away neatly with the hospital corners of the bedcovers she'd made.

They hadn't discussed what either of them expected to happen after last night but he'd have been more than happy to pick up where they'd left off. It was obvious they still had a fierce need burning for each other. One that went beyond all those barriers they'd both built up during their separation.

'You weren't here when I woke up.' She was still brushing down the already pristine covers, unable to meet his eyes, and it was obvious she'd assumed the worst. That he'd left her again without saying a word.

After everything they'd shared last night that simple lack of trust in him to do the right thing robbed him of some of his earlier euphoria. He'd opened himself up to her completely, probably more than he'd ever dared when they'd been together. Yet she still believed him capable of walking out on her again without a word. It reflected a little of what he'd put her through when she'd opted for that scenario rather than a more logical one. That protective hard shell she'd developed in his absence would take perseverance to break through but he was willing to put in the hard work to make her believe in him again.

'You were asleep. I only went out for this.' He showed her breakfast before setting it aside to move towards her.

'I, uh, thought you might have gone on without me.' A pair of red-rimmed, pain-filled eyes eventually faced him and ripped his heart in two. She'd been crying over him again, only this time without just cause. In future he was going to have to remember there'd been long-term consequences for his behaviour last year that weren't easily brushed aside simply because he'd finally got his act together. Freya needed time to recover and rebuild her trust exactly the same way he had.

'Hey, I was trying to do something nice for you.' He sighed but in keeping with the spirit of transparency in their relationship he decided to face the reason behind her apparent paranoia rather than leave it as the elephant in the room. 'I would never do that to you again.'

'I just… I couldn't go through that again. If last night was a one-off tell me now and get it over with.' She folded her arms across her chest and he could see her bracing herself for the truth above all else.

'Whatever happens from here on in I promise I'll always be honest with you.' He tugged her interwoven limbs apart, forcing her to open herself up to the possibility he'd changed, and pulled her towards him.

'So, what happens from here?' she muttered into his chest, still resisting as long as she could, but Lucas was determined that these last few private moments together should mark the start of their new beginning. He didn't want them flying back into limbo without having resolved everything once and for all.

'What do you want to happen?' He brushed her hair away from her neck and let his breath tickle the sensitive skin there until she was wriggling against him.

'That's not fair. You're playing dirty…' She was laughing now, a glorious sound after all the serious, often gut-wrenching conversations they'd shared recently.

'That's the idea.' He wanted to put the fun back in their relationship and remind them what they'd had before his dad had managed to ruin his life again.

'Lucas…' She tilted her face up, attempting to scold him, but a flirty half-smile played across her lips, tempting him towards more.

'I love you, Freya. I want to be with you. That's as honest as I can be and as much as I can give you right now.' He didn't want to talk about the practicalities when he'd thought too much about that the last time they'd been together. For once he wanted to live in the here and now, where nothing mattered beyond this little bubble.

She blinked, her eyes closing for a fraction too long, and it was clear she was mulling over what he was telling her. As much as he loved her, he couldn't promise her for ever. They'd both discovered to their cost that was a fallacy.

Then she opened her eyes and said, 'I love you too, Lucas.'

A year of pain and worry evaporated with those words he'd thought he'd never hear again. Love was something he'd taken for granted when they'd been together, but when he'd no longer had it in his life, there had been nothing on this earth capable of filling the void left behind.

He swooped on her lips, eager to reap the rewards of this reconnection and express how he felt about her without worrying about the consequences. They would work it out this time. Somehow.

Freya had instantly thought the worst when she'd realised Lucas had left without waking her and that a night with her had reminded him why he'd left in the first place. Especially when she'd wakened so full of hope that they could make another go at their marriage. In those paranoid moments alone in the igloo she'd considered if it had been better to have had that brief reunion, so full of honesty and passion, and risk her heart again than to have never have had any further knowledge of him at all. Even if he had gone on ahead to the hospital without her and flown home without an-other word, she could say with her hand on her heart it had been worth every second. Now he was here, reas-suring her he wasn't going anywhere for the foresee-able future, all those fears melted away against his lips.

This time there was no holding back as they stripped out of their clothes, eyes feasting on each other's naked flesh in the daylight of their admission as though they were truly seeing one another for the first time. He still loved her, she loved him and she couldn't see any rea-son why they couldn't be together and start over again.

That ray of hope was all she needed to justify reach-ing for Lucas again and letting her heart overrule her head. As she wrapped her arms around his neck and cushioned her body against his, he hitched her legs around his waist and carried her to one of the beds. His eyes never leaving hers, he laid her down on the mattress. Then he was kissing her all over so thor-oughly she couldn't think beyond where his mouth would land next.

His lips were soft, his mouth demanding, as he kneaded the tender skin on her inner thigh. That slow ascent towards her inner core left her aching with need for him inside her and that ultimate union of love and trust. He teased her with the tip of his tongue, mak-ing her wet with want, until she was arching from the bed and offering herself up to him for more. He filled her with one swift thrust, drawing her arousal straight through the centre of her body to meet him.

'I love you,' she cried out as he lapped her into that first burst of ecstasy so intensely it brought her to the brink of tears. It scared her how much Lucas still affected her body and mind and she only had his word he wouldn't shatter either again.

Then he shifted his body so he was prone against hers, his erection pressing insistently into her soft mound. Even though the evidence of his desire was straining to meet her, he moved slowly at first, answering that call inside her with one satisfying stroke. This was how it was supposed to be—so absorbed in one another it obliterated any of those dark thoughts that had hounded them in the past.

Freya ground her hips to meet Lucas's every thrust, urging him faster, deeper inside to drive out any lingering doubt about rekindling their relationship. That dizzying build-up of impending climax soon consumed her thoughts as well as her body, with Lucas's shallow breaths soon matching her own. They rose and fell together until his final roar of triumph rippled through his limbs and into hers. Freya rode it out with him until she couldn't hold back any longer, all of her pain finally expelled in the cry echoing around the walls.

Lucas didn't care that breakfast was cold or that he'd have one hell of a credit-card bill at the end of the month because this was the happiest he'd been in a long, long time. He and Freya had stayed wrapped in each other's naked limbs until visiting time had started at the hospital and they'd naturally prioritised Scarlett's welfare over their love life. Neither of them would neglect their professional duty in favour of their personal relationship. Once they were all safely home he and Freya would have all the time in the world for lazy mornings in bed, making love and getting to know each other again.

The hotel had arranged a lift for them, during which they'd barely been able to keep their hands off one another. Now they'd let down their emotional barriers it seemed as though they were physically trying to make up for lost time. Not that he was complaining. He'd spent too long without her and didn't want to waste any more time. If she was agreeable he'd move whatever belongings he had out of Pete's and back into the home where he belonged.

When they reached the hospital Freya offered to get Scarlett dressed so her weary parents could go and grab a coffee whilst Lucas checked with the staff that she'd been given her usual AEDs and all her obs were normal before they got their hopes up that she was able to go home.

'How are you feeling today, young lady?'

'I want to go home,' Scarlett insisted when he walked into her room, her forehead puckered into a frown and her lips pinched into a pre-tantrum pout.

'We'll get you there as soon as we can. I promise.' A quick check of her chart put Lucas's mind at ease that she was indeed ready to go so they didn't have a repeat of her last overtired tweenie performance.

'Just wait until you're doing this with your own kids and then the fun will really begin,' Freya whispered with good humour, but she might as well have jabbed him with a red-hot poker and jolted him out of his love-induced daze. He'd allowed himself to get lost in the fantasy of being with Freya again without considering the long-term consequences of his actions.

They might have faced up to the challenges of the past but ultimately it didn't change who they were as people or what they wanted from life. On that subject they remained poles apart. He still didn't want to take that chance he would follow in his father's footsteps, whilst Freya was born to be a mother.

Oblivious to the cold shower pouring down around them and extinguishing any hope of a future together, she was helping Scarlett into her outdoor clothes and fussing around her like a clucking mother hen. It was at that very moment he knew this was the end.

That mothering instinct blazing brightly in the room was a part of her, no one could deny. Not even him. No doubt that caring, empathetic side had been the key to unlocking that chamber of secrets he'd imprisoned himself in, away from her for so long. It wasn't going to change; she shouldn't *have* to change simply because he'd waltzed back into her life with his daddy issues.

As she buttoned Scarlett up to protect her from the elements and wiggled her boots onto her feet, it was easy to picture Freya doing the same for her own little girl someday. Although he still loved her and wanted to be with her so much it hurt, Lucas wasn't going to change his stance on having children. Not even mind-blowing sex could change the basic flaw in their marriage, which had been there even before his emotional meltdown.

The counselling and endless talking over what had happened might have propelled him through those childhood nightmares but the parenting hangover would last for ever. He wasn't taking the chance that his actions would impact for a lifetime on another small human. Even without his father's dark influences there were plenty of men who inadvertently hurt their children. He was damaged goods with a bad track record with those he loved and there was enough guilt and regret trailing in his shadow without adding more. Freya, her unborn children, and even he, would be better off if this ended here. Regardless of that emptiness already creeping back, eating away at him from the inside out. He knew how unbearable life was without her but it had to be preferable to condemning her to life without the family she obviously still wanted.

'You're a very lucky girl because you got an extra night in Lapland and that means extra Santa gifts.' He swallowed down his new heartache and produced the little snow globe he'd purchased in the hotel gift shop from his pocket.

'That looks just like the snowman at the airport!' Scarlett squealed with delight as she shook the dome and watched the snowflakes swirl around the glass.

'It's beautiful, Lucas.' Freya's appreciation meant he had to work extra-hard to gather his composure.

He'd bought it with her in mind—a token gift of their time together—but how could he possibly be so cruel as to give it to her now, knowing it would be a reminder of the end of their relationship for good? It was a tad traitorous to give it to another girl but he knew Freya would forgive him that, if nothing else.

As for the rest, there was nothing he could do or

say that was going to make up for what he was going to have to do to her for a second time.

Their time together had been a wonderful reunion of two lost souls finally finding one another in the dark again, but he had no more to offer her now than he had a year ago and he didn't want to make her believe otherwise.

Freya hugged her body tight against the cold, even though they'd long left the Arctic Circle behind. The atmosphere between her and Lucas had been decidedly chilly since they'd left the hospital, even though they'd managed to remain professional for Scarlett and her family. Deep down she'd known the magic wouldn't last for ever but she'd imagined they might at least make it home. It could've been that he was trying to maintain a personal distance for appearance's sake but that didn't account for his reluctance to make eye contact, or attempt any meaningful conversation about what was going to happen to them as a couple once they landed back in the real world. He was acting exactly the same way he'd been in those last days of their relationship and suddenly the tension Freya thought she'd rid herself of these past days was back in her body as she activated her self-defence mode once more.

They'd collected their luggage from baggage reclaim, filled in all relevant paperwork required for their unexpected extra night away and waved Scarlett and her much-relieved parents off home. She'd never dreamed this trip would've had such a personal impact.

Yet here she was, standing with her husband at the airport, not knowing what route they were taking next.

'I guess it's just us left now.' She had that washing machine swirling in the pit of her stomach, churning her insides on a speed wash. There hadn't been any semblance of an 'us' for hours now. Perhaps the Northern Lights had added a fairy-tale quality to their tryst that hadn't really been there at all or Lucas had got cold feet at the prospect of being her husband again. Whatever had brought about the sudden change in him, she wanted to be prepared for the fallout this time around. There was no point in living a lie together if he couldn't fully commit to her.

'Thank goodness we all got home in one piece in the end.' He hoisted his backpack onto his shoulder and lifted his overnight bag, leaving hers sitting where it was on the shiny airport floor. If he'd had any intention of leaving here with her, the gentleman in him would've undoubtedly offered to take her luggage too.

Someone opened the washing-machine door mid-cycle and left her slipping and sliding in the mess. Lucas might have made it here unscathed but her heart had definitely been damaged in transit.

He sneaked a glance at the exit and she knew he was getting ready to leave. At least the last time he'd taken the coward's way out he'd had his reasons. Well, she wasn't prepared to stand back and say nothing and spend the rest of her days not putting up some sort of fight.

'Did we? Or are we back to being two very different pieces going their separate ways again?' It took all of the strength she'd built up over the past year to keep the hysteria from her voice. She'd survived being an abandoned wife and she was pretty certain she'd get over being a fling for old times' sake, if this was all it had been to him, but she needed to know. There was no way she was wasting any more of her life waiting for him to make his mind up about what he wanted. She owed herself more than that.

'Freya…last night…this morning… It was a mistake.'

'Way to make a girl feel special,' she muttered as he crushed her last hope with a single word. Through her rose-tinted glasses it had been special, passionate, emotional and all the other positive feelings a woman would want to attach to a night with the man she loved. A *mistake* spoke of regret and remorse and all those negative connotations she didn't want him to associate with her.

He ditched his luggage again so all their baggage lay in a heap between them in the middle of the airport. It wasn't fair. In one of those far-fetched romantic films this should be the part where he declared his undying love for her and they walked off hand in hand. His sigh indicated this was going to be more of a bittersweet goodbye. The kind of heartbreaking tragedy you'd watch in bed with an unending supply of chocolate and tissues.

'It was amazing but does it really change anything between us? We still want different things. For you that's undoubtedly going to include a family and that's simply something I can't entertain. There's no point in either of us pretending this is going to work… In fact, we should probably see about getting a divorce. Then we can both move on.'

He stole her breath away with the blunt truth that she'd been asking for all along. Unfortunately, it wasn't the one she'd wanted to hear.

'Don't you think this is the kind of thing we should talk over in private?' It was true that desire to have another baby had probably dominated the early days of their marriage but that had been before their split, or Lucas sharing anything of his fears. She wouldn't bring another life into existence unless she was sure her relationship with the father was solid and this proved they were far from that ideal.

'Being with you this weekend and actually talking things through has helped me, it really has, but I think it's come too late for us.'

She wrenched away as he attempted to put his hands on her shoulders. He didn't get to touch her now if he was seriously going to dismiss what they'd had, what they'd shared, as if it had been any run-of-the-mill encounter.

'Well, I'm glad I could fix you and send you on your way.' The few words she managed to get out were dripping with bitterness towards the next woman he'd share his bed with but if he didn't think there was anything worth saving here then she wasn't going to beg him to change his mind. It had taken her long enough to claw back her dignity the last time he'd rejected her and she'd already proved she was strong enough to carry on without him. This was a setback but she'd bounce back again. It was what she did.

'I'm sorry, Freya. I only ever wanted to do the right thing by you.'

His platitudes were muted by the blood suddenly pounding in her ears as she grabbed her stuff and turned away. 'Don't forget those divorce papers. I think you know the address.'

The airport door swished open and she stepped outside with a confident stride. This was it, closure on Lucas Brodie and her ill-fated marriage. It had come at the cost of another very painful lesson about letting anyone that close enough to hurt her again.

As the cold air hit the tears on her face she swiped them away with the back of her hand. Thankfully she'd developed a thicker skin since last time.

CHAPTER SEVEN

FREYA WET SOME paper towels under the tap and pressed them to her flushed face and neck. It wouldn't be very professional to go back on the wards looking like this when she'd spent the best part of two months pretending to everyone she was fine. After a quick rummage in her purse, she popped a breath mint in her mouth and dabbed on some make-up to try to disguise the redness around her eyes. She stared at the reflection of the stranger in the bathroom mirror. Lapland with Lucas had changed her into someone she didn't recognise any more. She'd clearly underestimated the long-lasting effect spending time with him again would have on her and he'd left her with even more baggage to deal with than before.

The faint sound of Christmas carols filtered in from the wards and made her well up all over again. Whilst everyone else around her was gearing up to celebrate, they only served to remind her she'd been left alone and heartbroken for the season again.

When the wave of grief had passed and the puffiness around her eyes had subsided, she ventured outside into the corridor. Gillian was waiting, propped against the wall with her arms folded and her lips pursed.

'He really doesn't deserve any more of your tears.'

'Tell me something I don't know,' she muttered and kept on walking along the festooned corridor, somehow resisting the urge to rip down garish decorations.

There was no point in lecturing her now when the damage had been done.

'I'm serious. You can't let him get to you now when you'd been making such progress. I thought you'd both managed to get along when we were out there. What the hell happened after I left to have you in such a state?'

'Apparently nothing of any significance to him.' Freya hadn't shared the intimate details with anyone, in the naive belief it would help her forget more easily. She'd been so very, very wrong.

Gillian marched ahead, only to then spin around and force Freya to a complete stop. 'I wish I could get my hands on him. He swans off back to whatever cave he's been hiding in and leaves you picking up the pieces again. It's not right. He obviously must've made some sort of promise to you for you to be so cut up over him a second time.'

Now she thought about it, the only promise he'd actually made to her had been to be honest and not walk out on her again without an explanation. Well, he'd lived up to his word, brutally so. He'd told her he didn't want to be with her or have a family with her. Case closed.

Although Freya was tempted to incite her over-protective friend into bashing Lucas over the head with a bedpan on her behalf. It would be comedy gold if the whole thing wasn't such a disaster. The best of it was neither of them would understand why she was so upset.

'No promises. No blame anywhere except at myself.' It was her prerogative to stay mad at Lucas if she chose, but in the end, she'd had to take responsibility for her epic fail. She really should've known better.

'You can't spend every day crying in the ladies' toilets. You're making yourself ill. Don't think I haven't noticed you're hardly eating anything these days either.' Gillian assumed the role of nagging mother figure since Freya's own parents were happily far enough away they hadn't seen the evidence of her apparent decline for themselves. A tip-off that their only child wasn't eating properly and she'd be whipped back home and force-fed enough carbs to triple her dress size in no time.

At first she'd thought she'd been saved the humiliation of telling them she and Lucas were back together, only to have to admit he'd called it quits again. In another few months her increasing waistline and persistent single status were going to make it painfully clear what had happened anyway.

'I haven't had much of an appetite lately but I'll be fine. You don't need to worry.' The last thing she'd wanted was to draw attention to herself and imagined Gillian had only noticed something was wrong because she'd been looking for the signs. She'd witnessed the fallout from Lucas's unpredictable behaviour once before, so it was no wonder she in particular should be on her guard now.

'Why don't we get you seen by one of the doctors so they can give you something to lift your mood?' Gillian took her by the arm and for a second Freya thought she was actually going to drag her into one of the cubicles.

'There's nothing wrong with my mood. I would just like to get back to work. My break's over and I'm sure we've got a waiting room full of people out there.' There was sufficient drama in the halls of the emergency department every day of the week without adding hers to it. Medication wasn't going to change what had happened anyway.

'Will you stop being so stubborn and please just let me help you? Don't let him ruin your life again.' It was the concern in her friend's voice and that worried frown that finally broke her down. She'd tried to get through this on her own, with limited success, and it was only going to get tougher from here on in. A friend was the one thing she needed right now and that was all Gillian was trying to be for her.

'I won't.' The irony was he'd made her life worth living again after he'd left her with the most precious gift of all. Her guard slipped for a moment and her hands moved to protect the little souvenir growing in her belly.

Fate had brought the two of them together again that night and a lack of contraception had brought her a surprise not long after. Initially she'd put the nausea and unstable emotional state solely down to his rejection too, but she was a nurse; she'd figured it out eventually. As had Gillian apparently as she clocked the subtle movement and let out a shocked gasp.

Freya put her finger to her lips and moved her past the oversized Christmas tree and pile of brightly wrapped presents towards the empty triage room.

'You're pregnant?' Gillian might have done her best to keep the news quiet by mouthing the revelation but she had also grabbed Freya by both arms and was shaking her.

'You're going to make me throw up again if you keep doing that.' Her teeth were rattling but she was finally smiling again. It had been hard, keeping the news to herself, and at least with one confidante she might be able to enjoy this pregnancy. This baby hadn't got off to the easiest start with an absentee dad who'd made it clear a family wasn't in his plans for the future and a weeping mum mourning for her lost love. From here on her focus was going to be on the bundle of joy that would be arriving sometime in the summer.

'Sorry. Oh, come here.' Her friend pulled her into a bear hug and Freya couldn't help getting a tad emotional. The admission had relieved some of the stress from her shoulders now it wasn't a total secret.

'I can't believe I'm actually going to be a mum.' Telling Gillian somehow made it more real than the vomiting or the half-dozen pregnancy tests she'd taken to confirm those first suspicions. With that had come the parenting doubts that she was cut out for this on her own.

'Auntie Gillian will be there for scans and appointments and anywhere else you need me to hold your hand. That's if you want me getting in the way?'

'Of course I do.' Freya clutched her tighter, revelling in the friendship being extended to her and her unborn child. They were going to need all the help they could get. All the exciting stages of pregnancy might seem a tad less daunting as a single parent if she had someone by her side, taking an interest in the little jelly bean growing inside her.

'What about Lucas?' The hug disintegrated as Gillian broached the subject of the unwitting father-to-be and Freya moved back to reclaim her personal space.

'What about him?' Apart from his obvious part in the conception, this baby was nothing to do with her ex-husband. She didn't know how she was going to manage financially or emotionally with parenthood but Lucas not being part of it was the one thing she was sure about.

He'd confirmed it for her with a touching postcard from Lapland a few days after they'd returned, which she liked to look at in those moments of doubt she was doing the right thing by keeping him in the dark. It must've been posted the morning they'd visited the post office, before they'd spent the night together.

I could never be the family man you need me to be...

It would've been prudent if he'd told her that before they'd got married, or indeed before she'd slept with him again. The warning had come too late.

'He has a right to know.' Gillian's tone was much softer than before, probably because she knew she was treading on dangerous ground. Only a minute ago she'd been practically begging that the man be wiped completely from her memory.

'He doesn't have any rights. He wants a divorce.' That word was still a jagged needle piercing her skin every time it was mentioned. It was the legal confirmation her husband no longer wanted her and she had failed as a wife. No one got married thinking this was how it was going to end—living separate lives with a valley full of pain keeping them apart.

'Did he really say that?'

'Yes, he said that. So if you're harbouring any fantasies that a surprise pregnancy is somehow going to fix things you can get it out of your head now.' That had been her initial response too as those two little lines had appeared on the pregnancy test. Until common sense had kicked in and reminded her that married life had never lived up to her dream and it wasn't all going to fall into place now simply because she wanted it to.

The last time she'd seen him, the last words he'd spoken to her had made his position very clear. He didn't want her to be part of his life and a baby would tie them irrevocably together for ever. Neither of them wanted that. She knew she couldn't pretend for the rest of her life that she didn't have feelings for him if he did surprise her and insisted on fulfilling his duty to a child he didn't want. It would kill her to have to see him on a regular basis.

Their relationship had ended nearly a year ago and she'd convinced herself now that night had been a blip, a physical reconnection as a result of high emotions at

seeing each other again. A mistake after all. He'd probably assumed she was still on the pill since she hadn't
told him otherwise, and if she hadn't been feeling so
sorry for herself when she'd got home she might've
had time to do something to prevent this.

Except she didn't regret getting pregnant. She gently stroked her invisible bump, grateful for the blessing
inside. This was probably her only shot at motherhood
after swearing off men for life and she wanted to enjoy
every second of it.

'Okay. Okay. You know I don't have any love for
the man after everything he's done to you but as your
friend it's my duty to ask. From now on I won't say
another word about him.' She mimed locking her lips
and throwing away the key and managed to make Freya
smile again. Something she'd thought she would never
do after leaving Lucas at the airport. Even though she'd
had weeks of worry, this baby had likely saved her
from drowning in a pit of despair over her lost love.
She had a different focus now other than herself and
her broken heart, and a future to look forward to.

'Thank you. Now can I go and do my job? I can't
afford to be fired.' Every penny counted now she was
going to be a single parent and with the havoc this
pregnancy was already wreaking on her insides she
didn't know how long she'd be able to keep working.
As if to prove the point, her stomach contracted with
a sudden cramp, taking her breath away.

'Are you okay? Do you need to sit down?' Gillian
was already pulling a chair over for her but the sharp
pain was gone as quickly as it had arrived.

'I know this is early days but it's going to seem like a much longer pregnancy with you fussing all the time.' Freya brushed off the concern so she didn't go down the same line of thought. Cramps and sickness were part of the everyday experience of early pregnancy and she didn't want to stress herself out worrying that every little thing meant she would lose another baby.

'Tough. I'm in this with you.'

Another hug knocked the breath out of her as her new pregnancy partner physically demonstrated the strength of her support. Rather than push her away, Freya embraced the offer of help. For the first time since discovering her own little souvenir from Lapland, she no longer felt alone. Now the secret was out, she could start looking forward to the months ahead and plan her exciting new life as a single mother-to-be.

Lucas had received word that Sam, one of the little boys on the charity trip, had been admitted to the emergency department in Princes Street during the night after a severe asthma attack. Although not strictly one of his patients, he'd called in on his afternoon off to say hello and make sure he was all right. He'd stayed in touch with most of the families from that weekend, concerned with their progress after making a personal connection with those involved. Ironic when he'd been so afraid of committing to a family of his own.

That time with Freya and the children had shown him exactly what he'd been missing in his life but he'd panicked in the face of their strong-as-ever feelings for each other and had run away again rather than talk through his fears. They'd made a good team looking after the girls and they'd had fun together. There was no evidence he would end up anything like his father but he'd let the past take over again and steal Freya from him.

He'd stomped all over her trust by letting her down again and had made it impossible for her to forgive him. Now life seemed emptier than ever he knew the only mistake he'd made had been making a mess of the second chance she'd given him. These weeks apart had been soul-destroying, knowing it had been his own paranoia preventing him from being with her.

He knew he really had lost her for good this time but it didn't stop him lingering in her hospital territory in order to catch a glimpse of her.

He got his wish after he'd paid a visit to Sam on the main wards and he ran into her on the stairs.

'I…er…heard Sam had been admitted. Thought I'd check in on him.' Even though he'd anticipated seeing her again—had been reluctant to leave without doing so—he was a tad tongue-tied when they came face-to-face, as though he'd been caught doing something he shouldn't. After all, he'd been the one to put the brakes on any thoughts of a renewed attachment. If he truly thought they weren't right for each other he shouldn't have felt the need to look for her. He tried to justify his presence here with a valid, professional excuse.

'That's very kind. I was about to pop in myself, but on second thoughts I think I might leave it until later.' She turned and headed back the way she'd come as though she couldn't even bear to breathe the same air as him.

The hostile reception didn't come as a surprise after his recent behaviour but neither did it lessen the burden on his conscience. Every time he thought of how they'd left things at the airport he wanted to punch himself in the face for being so apparently blasé about it all, so it was only natural she wouldn't want to face him now. One night outside his comfort zone and those barriers he'd worked so hard to dismantle had been resurrected in double-quick time because he couldn't shake off that legacy of self-doubt his father had bestowed upon him.

'How are you, Freya?' He chose to ignore the snub and jogged after her in order to attempt a proper conversation. It wasn't merely small talk to ask about her health; she didn't actually look well. The shadows below her once sparkling eyes and paler-than-usual complexion were signs something was amiss. Despite her fiery demeanour there was a weariness surrounding her he could identify with after his own sleepless nights. He wasn't arrogant enough to suggest her thoughts should be entirely consumed by him but he was experienced enough in his own grief to read the telltale signs.

She stopped long enough to acknowledge him with a raised eyebrow, questioning the sincerity of his concern. It smarted as much as the open-palmed slap he'd expected. He still cared about her and that was exactly why he should have left things the way they had been between them. That night together had given them both false hope and caused even more damage than before. She'd told him exactly how much pain he'd put her through after the first break-up and he should never have given her false hope, knowing he couldn't fully commit. By making love to her and backing off he'd hurt her all over again. It was no wonder she could hardly bear to look at him.

'I'm fine,' she spat, taking sufficient time over the reply to warrant doubt.

'I'm not here for a fight, Freya. I just want to make sure you're all right.' He mentally strapped his hands to his sides to prevent him from reaching out to her.

'There's no need,' she insisted, and set off again without him.

It should've been his cue to walk the other way and end his responsibility to her here since she obviously didn't want to see or talk to him again, but he couldn't take his eyes off her when it might be the last time he saw her. He watched her descend quickly to the bottom of the stairs, chin in the air, back ramrod-straight with that same defensive guard back in place she'd had when they'd first met. The one that said, *Trust no one.*

His vigilance meant he saw her stumble when she reached the door, her hands clutching her stomach as she doubled over and had to lean against the wall for support.

'Freya?' He took the steps two at a time to reach her and slipped a hand around her waist to help keep her upright.

'Don't touch me.' She defied the pain she was clearly in to slap his hand away.

'Stop being so stubborn and let me help you.' He

might've failed as her husband but he was a doctor too and right now she needed medical assistance.

'I can manage on my own. I don't need…you.' The hiccup in her voice gave way to tears and Lucas's renewed sense of guilt kicked in. He was the reason she wouldn't accept help when she needed it most. Hadn't he done the same thing when his father had repeatedly hurt him until it had been too late? Freya shouldn't have to wait for whatever ailed her to spiral out of control because he'd made her afraid of letting anyone in again.

'I know you don't need me, you're stronger than anyone I know, but at least let me take you to see someone.' If she wasn't going to permit him to give his medical opinion, the least he could do was get her to someone she did trust enough to confide in. It was a pity he wasn't able to offer her the same support she'd provided for him but it was entirely his fault. He'd run out on her twice now, so why should she tell him anything about her life simply because they'd crossed paths now?

She snorted her derision at the apparent idea he knew anything about her now but even that minimal effort had her flinching again. Her legs seemed to buckle beneath her as she let out a sharp cry. Freya wasn't the sort of woman to show any weakness in public, especially not at work. There was something very, very wrong here and he wasn't taking any chances.

'What are you doing?' she gasped as he scooped her up into his arms with little effort.

'It'll be quicker than expecting you and your pride

to stagger back to the emergency department.' He wouldn't make any apologies for wanting to keep her safe, although she might not believe he had her best interests at heart.

'Stop it. You're causing a scene.' Even as she was reprimanding him, her face was contorted with pain and he knew he was doing the right thing. He could disappear once he'd got her the help she needed, if that was what she wanted, but he wasn't going to leave her here alone and in pain. Not this time.

'I'm sure they see husbands carrying their sick wives through here every day of the week.' He chose to ignore the small detail that she was in uniform because the only important element of this was to find out what was wrong with her and make her better.

'You're not my husband any more. You made that very clear. Please leave me to deal with this alone.' Her cries echoed in the corridor as she continued to resist his intervention. In the end, he had no choice but to set her back down on her feet before someone did see them and reported him for attempted kidnapping. The thought she hated him so much she would suffer rather than accept his help was a wake-up call to the damage he'd done. He certainly hadn't left her with the feel-good memories of the trip he'd intended by spending the night in that igloo.

At least they weren't too far from their destination and he insisted on accompanying her for the last few steps to get assistance.

'Can we get some help here, please?' he shouted at the staff who were congregated at the nurses' station, and led Freya into the nearest available cubicle. The acute pain in her abdominal region could be anything from appendicitis to a stress-induced ulcer caused by an insensitive ex-husband. In either case, she would need urgent treatment and he doubted she'd be inclined to take it from him.

He helped her onto the bed, and all the while she was crying out and clutching her side. That sense of helplessness he hadn't experienced since his break-down enveloped him. He wanted to fix everything for her but he didn't know how until they'd run all the tests they needed to diagnose the problem. She wouldn't even let him comfort her, the one thing he should be able to do for his wife.

He stepped out of the cubicle again to yell at the staff, who were already running towards him.

'Lucas?' Freya's shaky voice called him back in time to see a scarlet stain spreading across the centre of the white sheet covering the bed. This time she did reach out for him and he moved quickly to her bed-side, willing her to be all right.

'Everything's going to be okay, Freya.' He squeezed her hand to reassure himself as much as her. It was only now, faced with the prospect of something hap-pening to her, he could see what a fool he'd been in not making the most of every precious second he'd had with her.

'Please save my baby.' Her plea plunged straight into his chest cavity and ripped out his heart. She was pregnant? He swallowed down the sudden nausea rising in his belly to focus on comforting her as his brain tried to make sense of what was happening.

'You're in the best place to get help and I'm going to stay here with you.' He moved aside for the team to attend her, his role in supporting her emotionally much more important than trying to interfere in her treatment. She wasn't showing yet and if this was an early miscarriage there was little anyone could do other than keep her calm and make sure she rested.

'How far along are you, Freya?' The senior nurse bustled around, taking Freya's blood pressure, pulse and temperature, and ordered baseline bloods and a urine check in case of water infection. They were being as thorough as anyone could ask in the circumstances.

'About eight weeks…'

The mental calculations almost had Lucas sinking onto the hospital bed beside her. Unless she'd hooked up with someone else immediately before or after their night together, which he highly doubted, this baby was his.

He hadn't given a thought to contraception when they'd been together in Lapland, so this was a possibility he should've considered. Not that it made any difference to what Freya was going through now.

He knew losing a baby would crush her even more than he already had by leaving her. It wasn't her fault, or the baby's, that he'd messed up. He knew what it was to suffer for the mistakes of the parents and he wouldn't inflict the same unjustifiable punishment on another generation.

'I can't go through this again,' she managed to get out between sobs.

He'd barely had time to contemplate being a father and now it seemed as though fate would steal it away from him. Equally horrific, it appeared Freya had gone through this before. Probably alone. It was no wonder she hated the sight of him if he'd caused this to happen twice.

'They're just going to take some blood samples. I know it's hard but try to get some rest.' If he could take her pain or fears away he would, when she'd gone through so much since marrying him. He couldn't hold it against her that she'd kept the news from him when he'd been so vehemently against the idea of a family the last time they'd been together.

Now it was going to be an anxious wait for both of them to find out if this was still a viable pregnancy. The outcome of this day could very well change his life for ever, and while fatherhood mightn't have been something he'd wanted or planned, this baby was a part of him and Freya. Fate had stepped in when he'd made a mess of their relationship and had made the decision for him to be a father. Now they were linked together for the rest of their lives.

He pictured the little bundle of their DNA, with Freya's big brown eyes and warm smile, and he couldn't help but love it already.

Freya wrapped her arms around her stomach, praying that willpower alone could somehow keep her baby safe in there as she was wheeled to the early pregnancy unit. Lucas must've had a hundred questions since she'd dropped the baby bombshell, including asking for confirmation that he was the father, but he'd been calm and supportive so far.

It could've been merely his excellent bedside manner keeping him here with her, but he'd been the one to pull a few strings and get her transferred to the unit for this ultrasound to put her mind at rest that the baby was okay. He'd barely let go of her hand since the cramps had taken hold and she didn't want him to. Even though they'd split in less-than-ideal terms, there was no one else she wanted with her through this. She still loved him and despite all his protestations about becoming a father she had seen the worry on his face for their unborn child and wanted him to want this baby as much as she did.

Tears began to pour down her face at the familiar sight of the tinsel-lined corridors and thoughts of the last time she'd been wheeled through here on the way to discover the fate of her unborn child.

After the devastating discovery at the scan of her first miscarriage they'd told her what would happen to her body as nature took its course over the following weeks but no one had warned her how much she would mourn the child she had never got to meet. It had taken her a long time to stop hating those people who'd told her she was young and could always have another, as if any loved one was as easily replaced as an empty milk carton. Or to stop the overwhelming jealousy and sense of injustice every time someone else gave birth to a healthy baby when she hadn't. She wouldn't survive a loss a second time when becoming a mother was the one thing keeping her going since she and Lucas had parted ways.

The cramps and bleeding had stopped before she'd been moved from the emergency department but this interminable wait for the ultrasound was hell. So much worse than waiting for those lines to appear on the pregnancy test in the first place. She knew all too well what she was in for if the worst happened—sad faces, apologies and going home without her baby.

Lucas rested his hand on hers and gave her a gentle squeeze. 'Try and relax. All the tests came back to say everything was fine.'

'I know but I don't want to go into that room with false hope, only to see that look on the sonographer's face that says something's wrong.' Freya would never forget lying on that bed alone, a growing unease when the technician had left the room, and the devastation when she'd brought someone else back to break the bad news that there was no heartbeat. That there would be no baby.

'Do you want me to come in with you?' Lucas made the offer as she waited for her name to be called and she clung to it the same way she was trying to cling to her pregnancy.

'Would you?'

'Of course. This is my baby too. Right?' There was still that air of hesitancy about his role, which could be attributed to the fact neither of them had acknowledged it thus far.

'Right. I'm sorry I didn't tell you but I thought in the circumstances… Your postcard came a few weeks ago…' Until now she'd thought the contents of his note had said everything he thought about the subject of fatherhood. Now, after spending the afternoon taking care of her and fretting with her, she wasn't sure what to believe.

He frowned and she could see him trying to figure out what she was talking about. Then he formed an 'O' with his mouth and shook his head. 'Sorry. I was trying to be honest with you but as usual I've only succeeded in making things worse.'

'Did you mean it?' She had a lot of explaining to do with regard to both pregnancies she'd kept secret from him, but she didn't see the point of putting herself through that if this was all for show. He had to decide once and for all if he was in this with her or not.

'I did. At the time.' The matter no longer seemed so clear cut for Lucas any more.

'And now?'

'I don't want to lose either of you.' The sudden truth hit him as he rested his eyes on the wife he loved so very much and thought of the baby they'd already created. It had taken the shock of potentially having his family taken from him to realise it was what he wanted after all. He just prayed it wasn't too late.

The arrival of the sonographer and the prep for the scan soon concentrated all their fears into one place. The room was silent as they waited for the all-clear and he swore they'd all stopped breathing in order to hear the heartbeat clearly and know beyond doubt the baby was still okay.

'There we go. Normal embryo development for this stage and the lovely strong heartbeat I'm sure you were waiting to hear.' The confirmation that she was still pregnant almost brought him to his knees with gratitude for the chance he'd been given to step up and be a father to this baby.

'Thank you.' His voice cracked with the swell of unexpected emotion at the news.

Huge sobs racked Freya's small frame as she shared his relief and he gathered her into his arms and hugged her close to his chest. As he held her tight and stroked her hair he desperately wanted to make things right. Even if she couldn't bring herself to trust him again she needed someone at her side, supporting her through this pregnancy.

'It's been a long, stressful day for you, Freya. Go home and make sure you get plenty of rest.' The sonographer dished out the same advice she'd been given in the emergency department. She needed to take it easy. It was still early days and they wouldn't want to take any more chances of something going wrong with this pregnancy.

'I'll try,' she promised as she detached herself from his arms, that stubborn streak already rebelling against the idea of help.

'You'll do more than try and I'm going to make sure of it.' He frowned at her, unwilling to let her shut him out when she was going to need him most. That little heartbeat had overridden those fears about becoming a father to make him focus on what was important. The safety of his blossoming family.

'Oh? And how are you going to do that?'

'Easy. I'm moving back home until you've had this baby.'

CHAPTER EIGHT

FREYA TOOK ANOTHER deep breath in and counted to ten as they pulled up outside the house. She was trying to keep calm for the sake of the baby but Lucas wasn't making it easy with this ridiculous plan. It was guilt talking, she knew that, and the only reason she'd let him take it this far was so she could get home quicker. She had to prioritise bed rest over personal feelings when getting into an argument now would only send her blood pressure sky-high.

There was nothing she wanted more than to have him back, raising this baby, with her but not through a sense of duty. If it had been anything more than that, he'd had plenty of opportunity to tell her.

'Thanks for the lift.' All she wanted to do was climb into her bed and alternately thank her lucky stars and feel sorry for herself. Today had brought back a lot of unhappy memories and worry, not to mention the over-whelming relief to still be coming home as a mother-to-be. The effort of it all had left her bone weary.

'I told you, you don't have to go through this on your own.' There was still no sign of any emotional attachment beyond his sense of obligation and even if there had been it would take a lot for her to believe in him again.

By the time she'd got out of the car he'd already opened the front door. She'd forgotten he still had a key. In the naive hope he'd arrive home during those early days of his absence she'd been afraid to change the locks. Now it seemed as though he was quite happy to waltz in as though nothing had happened and take over. She wasn't up for another fight but Lucas pretending he wanted to be part of this was just as bad as not having him in her life, if not worse. It certainly wouldn't make him love her any more—in fact, he'd probably come to resent her for trapping him into a relationship of sorts.

'I am in this on my own. I have been for quite some time in case you've forgotten.' She pushed past him into the house they'd once shared, not really prepared for the sight of him here again in very different circumstances from those she'd ever imagined.

'There's nothing I can do to change the past but I will be here for you and the baby if you'll let me. I know that neither of us planned this, but you still need to take it easy and I'm looking for a place to stay, so this seems like the ideal solution to me.' He tossed his keys onto the table in the hallway just as he always had, so casually an outsider would've sworn he'd never been away. If she'd stockpiled the forest's worth of handkerchiefs she'd cried into, they would tell a different story, but she'd long since picked herself back up and no longer lay around waiting for him to save her from her misery.

'That all sounds very practical but I can manage. This doesn't have to affect you at all.' Today had been a wake-up call. She didn't need stress in her life and that included dealing with an ex who'd never wanted to be a father. The baby came first and she was planning on taking some sick leave until the danger period had passed and even then she might cut back her hours.

Lucas plumped up some of the cushions on the couch and guided her towards a seat, as though he'd just started working in an old people's home. This wasn't the heart-warming return of her husband she'd once dreamed of—it was an act of pity.

'I couldn't be more affected. I'm going to be a father.' He waited until she sat down before he presented his argument. Although he didn't raise his voice, the furrow in his forehead and the careful delivery of his words had her flinching all the same.

In all the scenarios she'd run in her head this wasn't how she'd imagined he would find out either. A threatened miscarriage had barely given him time to get used to the idea of becoming a father before all hell had broken loose. Still, she didn't want the drama to cloud his judgement on the matter when he'd been so adamant he hadn't wanted to start a family with her.

'You don't have to be. I was fully prepared to do this on my own. Just walk away and forget about it. You're good at that.' Now the immediate threat of losing her baby had passed, she was preparing to go into emotional lockdown again. There was no point in letting him get close again, only for him to run when he realised this life wasn't for him. The next time there'd be more than her feelings hurt.

Instead of storming out and slamming the door behind him, which she'd expected and almost hoped for, he sat down on the seat beside her. 'I haven't behaved well towards you, I know that, but I want to make it up to you. I can take you to appointments, help get the house ready for the little one coming, pay the bills, do all the things a partner should do.'

Except love her. That was something that he couldn't seem to force himself to do. She didn't want to play house. It would be too painful when she couldn't have him in her life as more than an obligated father to her baby.

'All the things I can do on my own.' It wasn't going to be easy but she would manage somehow. Time and again she'd found out the hard way she couldn't rely on anyone except herself.

'This house is still half mine, Freya. I could just move back but I want us to work together as a team on this. Look, I'll move out once the baby's safely here if that's what you want. Just let me help.' There was probably a legal argument against it since he'd effectively abandoned her and said 'house' but she knew it was only a matter of time before she caved. Partly because he looked so utterly adorable and sincere but mostly because deep down she knew that was what she wanted.

'I'm tired and I'm scared, Lucas. If I agree to this it's only for the baby's sake. You don't get to interfere in my life. Think of it as a supporting role rather than the lead man.' She needed to protect herself emotionally if they were going to be under the same roof again. They needed clear boundaries so they didn't repeat the mistakes of the past and she could protect what was left of her shattered heart.

'That's fine with me.'

She'd known it would be. After all, it wasn't really her he felt duty-bound to protect. If that had been the case, he would've come back long ago. Her vision blurred with tears and she knew she had to leave before she frightened him off again with actual feelings.

'You know where the spare room is.' He was a lodger now and it was best she start to see him that way. Which might be easier if she moved all his things out of the bedroom they'd once shared. His shirts still hung in the closet for the same reason she'd never changed the locks: she'd still held out that hope for a reconciliation. Just not one like this—where he'd been trapped into it and she was as unhappy and lonely as ever.

'I've made you some vegetable soup and crusty bread. There's even some chocolate cake for dessert.' Lucas balanced the tray on one hand whilst he knocked gently on Freya's door and tried to coax her out with some comfort food.

She needed plenty of bed rest but it wouldn't be healthy for her to confine herself completely to her room if he moved in. He wanted one last chance to prove how much he loved her and to make a go of their marriage, but she was so fragile at the minute, and skittish around him, he didn't want to push her. After everything he'd done she had no reason to trust him but he would be here for her in whatever capacity she would have him. Even if it was only as a chauffeur or home help. Anything was better than spending the rest of his days without her in his life.

'Thanks.' She opened the door wide enough to take the tray and for him to see how pale she was, defying the idea of that mythical pregnancy bloom.

'Are you okay? You're not queasy or having pains again?' He hoped she would tell him if that was the case but since she hadn't seen fit to even confide in him about the pregnancy he wasn't so sure.

'No. Just tired.' It was obvious the attempt at a smile was for his benefit, to get him off her back, but it only managed to deepen his frown. The lack of communication and fractured trust was a side effect, not merely from his illness but also from his continued mishandling of their relationship. In trying to control the situation and prevent the worst from happening, he'd steered them into an even bigger mess. If he didn't want to end up a replica of his father he was going to have to step up and fix things, instead of leaving them to fester out of control.

Which was difficult to do when he was staring at the closed door again, Freya having retreated into her cave with her food like some sort of frightened animal.

He rested his forehead on the cool wood, trying to come up with a solution. As a doctor it was his job to treat the symptoms of an illness but this was about much more than a physical ailment. Freya was unhappy and frightened about the future. He needed something to convince her she could trust him to be there for her and there was one obvious treatment to help get her back to her happy, smiling best. Christmas.

It was only a couple of weeks away, and though he was happy to let the season pass him by without as much as writing a card, Freya in December without tinsel was like Lapland without snow. It simply wasn't the same.

Lucas wrestled the Christmas tree into a bucket in the middle of the living room, sweat running down his back and pine needles pricking every inch of available skin. It had been the biggest, bushiest tree on the lot and he'd picked it specifically because of its close resemblance to those they'd seen in Lapland. Now he'd cut it free of its bindings and the limbs had sprung free, he wondered if he'd been *too* sentimental in his choice. Although Freya had always insisted there could be no such thing as over-enthusiasm at Christmas, it wouldn't come as any surprise if he'd discover a family of woodland animals living in the swaying branches of this majestic beauty. It would certainly make an impact on Freya and that was all he wanted.

His single begrudged contribution during their one Christmas together here had been the heavy lifting of decorations from the attic, so he continued his quest there. One by one he carried the boxes of Freya's treasured baubles down the ladder and into the living room, with a greater deal of optimism than the last time. By that stage he'd already been struggling to come to terms with the news of his father's death and questioning his own suitability as a family man. It was ironic now that impending fatherhood should bring him back.

He didn't know what kind of dad he was going to make, which was why he'd been afraid to take the risk of finding out. That decision had since been taken out of his hands. Even if he was financially supportive, or a physical presence in his child's life, there was no guarantee he'd be able to give that emotional support he'd never received from his parents but he was certainly willing to try. The one thing he was certain of was that Freya would make the best mum. She simply needed a little help to enjoy the pregnancy.

He ripped the tape off the boxes with an enthusiasm he'd never experienced around the season and it was all for her benefit. The amount of glittery fairies and snow-dusted teddy bears surrounding him was quite overwhelming but he vaguely remembered these were the 'room' decorations and set about filling every available furniture space with the oddities. The six-foot artificial pine tree lying in the corner of the attic with its bent branches and the remnants of a few broken ornaments still attached had seen better days. Although it confirmed he'd made the right decision in buying a real tree, images of Freya struggling up the ladder to pack away the decorations alone whilst he had been holed up in his friend's apartment pricked his conscience.

The uncared-for symbol of her emotions last year

disturbed him more than the over-the-top nod to a childhood he'd only dreamed of ever could. He'd never understood the whole build-up to one day because he hadn't experienced that excitement himself. It had just been the same as every other day in his house, only perhaps with added disappointment. Freya, on the other hand, craved it, or at least she had until he'd tainted the memory of it. She needed this more than ever.

He was out of his depth in the tangle of fairy lights and tinsel but he draped them around the branches as best he could. It might not win any style awards but as he stood back to admire his handiwork he was quite proud of the display. Even he had to admit it brightened up an otherwise dull December day.

'What on earth are you doing?' a bemused Freya said from behind him.

He stood aside so she could enjoy the full effect of his efforts. 'Christmas isn't far away. I thought we should put a few decorations up to mark the occasion.'

'A few? It looks like an explosion in a tinsel factory.' The corners of her mouth tilted up as she took in the scene and made it all worth it.

'I thought that was the style you preferred?' He risked a little teasing back, hoping to encourage her back to her usual sparky self.

'Believe it or not, there is some order called for when it comes to Christmas decoration. Symmetry is usually a good place to start.' Freya advanced towards the wonky tree and began to rearrange the ornaments and lights, which even Lucas had to agree he'd

chucked on rather than placed with any sort of preci-
sion. The criticism didn't bother him when it seemed
he'd achieved the purpose of getting her to interact
with the world outside her bedroom again.

'You're the expert. I'm still on the beginner's level.'
In more areas than just tree decorating.

'I can't believe you went out and bought a real tree.
You always complained about the mess they made…'

He'd been in too much turmoil to be bothered with
the hassle then but seeing her happy made a valuable
argument for going to all the trouble.

'I'm a different man from the one I was then. I
wanted you to see that.' Lucas wanted to show her he'd
do anything to make her happy, that she could trust
him again. More than that, he wanted to convince her
this time he was back for good.

As she watched his attempt to decorate the tree, Freya
wondered if it wasn't doing her more harm than good
to have Lucas here, pretending she could count on him.
His gesture was so thoughtful it hurt but she kept asking herself why he would do such a thing if he was only
here to save face. No one but the two of them would
ever know he'd done this, not even the baby, unless
they made it into an anecdote someday. Hope bubbled
inside her that this was his way of proving his com-
mitment to her with the one thing she loved almost as
much as him.

'You never did this with your mother?' She handed
him another box of decorations before she started

blubbing again and he wouldn't be able to distinguish her happy tears from all the rest.

Of course she knew now of the strained relationship he'd had with his father but she'd heard nothing about his mother beyond the fact she'd abandoned him when he'd been little. It seemed almost Dickensian that no one should ever have shown him the simple joys of Christmas, such as hanging baubles on a tree or sledding down a hill in the snow, yet he was as awkward in these activities as she was enthusiastic.

He paused as he hung the blue and white snowflake her gran had crocheted for her on his side of the tree.

'I might've done when I was very young but I don't remember much about her at all other than my father's temper and drinking getting worse after she left.' He shrugged his shoulders and continued to upset her sense of visual balance.

It was no wonder she'd had such a hard time persuading him this was fun when the only memories he had associated with the season were probably tied to a sense of loss and gave his actions now more meaning than ever. He was doing this to give her something to look forward to, to take her mind off anything other than happy thoughts, even though it would be a huge personal challenge for him. He was putting her first.

'Is that why you're here now? For the baby?' She wanted him to spell it out for her so there would be no misunderstanding on either side. If this was about proving himself and abandonment issues he'd never fully explored, she'd rather know upfront instead of waiting to find out eight months down the line and have her heart broken again. It was obvious to her she was still in love with him when it had hurt so much to see him today and that he was still the only one she'd wanted with her when she'd thought she was going to lose the baby. Then again, she'd never actually stopped loving him. She doubted she ever would.

'I'm here for both of you.' He reached over and gave her a half-hug, the first body contact they'd had since he'd comforted her in the hospital. It could've been her hormonal imagination but the gesture seemed to last longer than a mere show of solidarity ought to. There was time for his warmth to seep into her skin and somehow make her feel as though he really could protect her from all the bad stuff. When he did let go he kept his gaze centred on the tree rather than anywhere near her and she wanted to believe it was because he'd felt that connection again too. Just like the one they'd had in the igloo when their world had been each other and nothing else had mattered.

'What's this one? I don't remember seeing this before.' Lucas picked up the little porcelain angel that held so much importance to her.

She could've played down its significance the way she'd done last year when she'd purposely left it in the box. By consigning her heartache to the past and focusing on a future, she'd believed they'd had, she'd thought she'd be able to move past the pain. The ensuing months of misery had shown her otherwise. Lucas had confronted his demons and it was about time she did the same.

'I bought this for the baby I lost.' She took the angel

dangling from his index finger and hung it on the front of the tree, where she would see it every day.

Lucas watched it swinging on the tree in a reverent silence that Freya appreciated. Not everyone around her had been as respectful of her loss at the time. As though the early miscarriage somehow hadn't counted as the death of a child. It had felt traumatic enough to a young girl who'd been carrying the much-wanted baby.

'Was it my fault? Did it happen when I left?' he asked finally, clenching his hands into fists as he shared his unwarranted fears over something that had happened long before he'd ever been on the scene.

Freya shook her head. 'No. I was only eighteen when I fell pregnant the first time. We were engaged, I thought we were in love, but he ran out on me the second he found out. I don't know if it was the stress that caused the miscarriage but I guess it was something I never really got over. In hindsight, perhaps my enthusiasm to start a family with you as soon as we were married was my way to get past the tragedy of losing my baby so young. I should never have rushed you into a place you weren't ready to go.'

'I wish you'd told me.' The tenderness in his voice made her question her decision not to tell him from the start, but they'd both made mistakes in those early days of their marriage. With a baby on the way they were going to have to be more mature than ever about how they handled such important issues.

'I should have, I'm sorry, but it was part of my life I simply didn't want to revisit. Everyone told me I was young, I'd get over it in time, and I foolishly believed

I really could leave the past behind. It seems we have a lot more in common than we ever realised. Perhaps if we'd both been a bit more honest about our feelings we could've made it through the last year together.' She dared say what she hoped he was thinking. It wasn't the first time she'd wondered where they might be if they'd been able to talk to each other, rather than internalising the baggage they'd brought into the marriage.

'I thought I'd caused you to lose the baby. That you'd never forgive me.' There was a sadness in his eyes as he met hers that made her heart give a little flip. If there was the slightest hope they could still make a go of their marriage, she wanted to seize hold of it and nurture it just like she would their baby.

'Now you know the truth and there's no reason for you to feel guilty, how do you feel about this baby? And me?' There was an involuntary gulp before her last question because she couldn't quite believe she was asking it. She was done pretending if there was a chance of having this for real and they let it slip away for the sake of pride or fear, or whatever reasons they'd had in the past for not coming clean with one another. Whether he wanted to be with her, or he was here for the baby only, she needed to know so she could prepare herself for the future.

'I love you, Freya. I always have. I know it might not have seemed it at times but I've never stopped loving you. Everything I've done… I was trying to protect you.'

'From what?'

'Me.'

'That's the mistake you keep making, Lucas. I'm not some fragile, defenceless damsel who needs saving and neither are you the villain of the piece. I want to be with you for *you*. I love *you*. All I need to know in return is that you love me and you're going to be here for me. For us.'

'I'm scared I'll turn out like *him*. That I won't be enough.' Finally he let her see inside his soul where those fears were so deep rooted they'd nearly suffocated the life out of him.

'You've always been enough. You just have to believe in yourself.' She took his hand and placed it gently on her midriff and for the first time let herself imagine the three of them as a happy family.

'I might need your help with that.' There was a genuine plea behind the joking facade that Freya couldn't ignore. He was being honest in admitting his fears and asking for her support this time. If she didn't reciprocate that level of trust and believe he'd be there for her in return, they may as well call it quits now. They were both going to have to have faith that they could make it work this time. Although they might have faltered as a couple, they both had to accept the blame for expecting too much the first time around.

'You're going to make the best dad. I know it.' Of that she had no doubt. She'd seen it from the first time they'd worked together on the children's ward and he'd proved it in his continuing care for the youngsters on the Lapland trip. His actions today, and his spontaneous tree purchase, already showed the love he had for her and his unborn child in trying to make Christmas happen.

'I'm really going to be a dad.' He smoothed his hand tenderly over her flat-for-now belly as he came to terms with impending fatherhood, and she knew this baby would finally help love triumph over fear. He was beginning to look towards a future, instead of letting the past keep him chained away from her and everything else that could make him truly happy.

'Yes, you are, and I'm going to be a mum.'

Although there was still a long way to go, that kind of positive thinking and acceptance was exactly what they needed to heal and grow together. Now they'd dealt with the past, this baby was the beginning of a new chapter in their lives—the fresh start they both needed.

She rummaged in the box for a plastic sprig of mistletoe to hold above their heads and seal their new vows to each other in a kiss.

This time she knew love would be enough.

EPILOGUE

One year later

'IF YOU CAN just straighten Reuben's hat, this will be perfect.' Lucas directed his subjects from behind the camera, having become quite the photographer in the months since his son's birth.

'Tell me we're not going to be one of those smug families that sends cheesy Christmas cards of themselves.' Freya adjusted Reuben's green elf hat, which matched her own, but she knew they couldn't hold the pose for ever, no matter how perfect he wanted the shot.

'And why not? I'm very proud of my family.' There was no disputing his claim as the snap-happy father set the timer on his tripod-steadied camera and made a dash into the frame, wearing one of the many ugly Christmas sweaters he'd taken to wearing recently.

The baby, who wasn't to know better, was particularly fond of this particular reindeer jumper with the flashing red nose, but Freya was certain Lucas's sudden enthusiasm for the season wasn't solely for the little one's benefit. He couldn't yet read the embroidered stockings hanging from the mantelpiece, which his daddy had bought for all three of them.

She almost daren't think it but it was possible Lucas was looking forward to Christmas and sharing it with his family as much as she was.

The camera flashed at the exact second their baby elf threw up all over his cute outfit.

'Don't worry, I'll sort it.'

Before she even had to lift a finger, Lucas was there, scooping Reuben into his arms for a much-needed clean-up.

Despite all his fears about becoming a dad, he'd been amazing, doting on his son the way a new father ought to, as well as making up to her for lost time. Their relationship had certainly benefitted from their new honesty policy now there was nothing holding them back from trusting each other, or themselves. They'd both found a certain peace in parenthood, which had gone some way to diluting the pain of the past when they had such a bright future to look forward to together. Starting with their first Christmas at home.

She wanted to make it as special for Lucas as he'd made it for her.

'Any idea what you want Santa to bring this year?' She fished for some gift ideas as he played peeka-boo with the baby on the changing mat. This year she had more reason than ever to go over the top and she couldn't wait to go on a spending spree to show her appreciation for everyone she had in her life.

Lucas paused as he thought about it. Then he turned

to her and she recognised that picture of perfect contentment on his face because it was the same expression she saw in the mirror every day. 'I don't need anything else. I have everything I need right here.'

'Me too.' In that second the need for all the fancy trimmings around her evaporated because she knew he was right. The sight of her husband playing with her son was all she needed to make her happy. Family was the only thing that mattered, and now they had one of their own, life was complete.

It really was going to be the best Christmas ever.

* * * * *

*If you enjoyed this story, check out
these other great reads from Karin Baine*

*REFORMING THE PLAYBOY
FALLING FOR THE FOSTER MUM
THE COURAGE TO LOVE HER ARMY DOC
THE DOCTOR'S FORBIDDEN FLING*

All available now!

MILLS & BOON®
Hardback – November 2017

ROMANCE

The Italian's Christmas Secret	Sharon Kendrick
A Diamond for the Sheikh's Mistress	Abby Green
The Sultan Demands His Heir	Maya Blake
Claiming His Scandalous Love-Child	Julia James
Valdez's Bartered Bride	Rachael Thomas
The Greek's Forbidden Princess	Annie West
Kidnapped for the Tycoon's Baby	Louise Fuller
A Night, A Consequence, A Vow	Angela Bissell
Christmas with Her Millionaire Boss	Barbara Wallace
Snowbound with an Heiress	Jennifer Faye
Newborn Under the Christmas Tree	Sophie Pembroke
His Mistletoe Proposal	Christy McKellen
The Spanish Duke's Holiday Proposal	Robin Gianna
The Rescue Doc's Christmas Miracle	Amalie Berlin
Christmas with Her Daredevil Doc	Kate Hardy
Their Pregnancy Gift	Kate Hardy
A Family Made at Christmas	Scarlet Wilson
Their Mistletoe Baby	Karin Baine
The Texan Takes a Wife	Charlene Sands
Twins for the Billionaire	Sarah M. Anderson

MILLS & BOON®
Large Print – November 2017

ROMANCE

HISTORICAL

MEDICAL

MILLS & BOON®
Hardback – December 2017

ROMANCE

His Queen by Desert Decree	Lynne Graham
A Christmas Bride for the King	Abby Green
Captive for the Sheikh's Pleasure	Carol Marinelli
Legacy of His Revenge	Cathy Williams
A Night of Royal Consequences	Susan Stephens
Carrying His Scandalous Heir	Julia James
Christmas at the Tycoon's Command	Jennifer Hayward
Innocent in the Billionaire's Bed	Clare Connelly
Snowed in with the Reluctant Tycoon	Nina Singh
The Magnate's Holiday Proposal	Rebecca Winters
The Billionaire's Christmas Baby	Marion Lennox
Christmas Bride for the Boss	Kate Hardy
Christmas with the Best Man	Susan Carlisle
Navy Doc on Her Christmas List	Amy Ruttan
Christmas Bride for the Sheikh	Carol Marinelli
Her Knight Under the Mistletoe	Annie O'Neil
The Nurse's Special Delivery	Louisa George
Her New Year Baby Surprise	Sue MacKay
His Secret Son	Brenda Jackson
Best Man Under the Mistletoe	Jules Bennett

MILLS & BOON®
Large Print – November 2017

ROMANCE

An Heir Made in the Marriage Bed	Anne Mather
The Prince's Stolen Virgin	Maisey Yates
Protecting His Defiant Innocent	Michelle Smart
Pregnant at Acosta's Demand	Maya Blake
The Secret He Must Claim	Chantelle Shaw
Carrying the Spaniard's Child	Jennie Lucas
A Ring for the Greek's Baby	Melanie Milburne
The Runaway Bride and the Billionaire	Kate Hardy
The Boss's Fake Fiancée	Susan Meier
The Millionaire's Redemption	Therese Beharrie
Captivated by the Enigmatic Tycoon	Bella Bucannon

HISTORICAL

Marrying His Cinderella Countess	Louise Allen
A Ring for the Pregnant Debutante	Laura Martin
The Governess Heiress	Elizabeth Beacon
The Warrior's Damsel in Distress	Meriel Fuller
The Knight's Scarred Maiden	Nicole Locke

MEDICAL

Healing the Sheikh's Heart	Annie O'Neil
A Life-Saving Reunion	Alison Roberts
The Surgeon's Cinderella	Susan Carlisle
Saved by Doctor Dreamy	Dianne Drake
Pregnant with the Boss's Baby	Sue MacKay
Reunited with His Runaway Doc	Lucy Clark

MILLS & BOON®

Why shop at millsandboon.co.uk?

Each year, thousands of romance readers find their
perfect read at millsandboon.co.uk. That's because
we're passionate about bringing you the very best
romantic fiction. Here are some of the advantages
of shopping at www.millsandboon.co.uk:

* **Get new books first**—you'll be able to buy your
  favourite books one month before they hit
  the shops

* **Get exclusive discounts**—you'll also be able to buy
  our specially created monthly collections, with up
  to 50% off the RRP

* **Find your favourite authors**—latest news,
  interviews and new releases for all your favourite
  authors and series on our website, plus ideas for
  what to try next

* **Join in**—once you've bought your favourite books,
  don't forget to register with us to rate, review and
  join in the discussions

Visit **www.millsandboon.co.uk**
for all this and more today!